She did tricky little things to his mind and wreaked havoc with his body. The two weeks that she was scheduled to stay at the hotel couldn't pass quickly enough as far as he was concerned.

Two weeks. Then Andrea would repack her suitcase, settle her bill and leave. She'd be gone, never to be seen again.

Never? his mind echoed.

Well, sure. That was how it was with guests of the hotel. They came, they went, end of story. Unless Andrea decided to visit Prescott again at some point in the future and stayed at Hamilton House while doing so, in two weeks she'd be out of sight, out of mind forever.

Wrong, Brandon thought in the next instant. He had a sneaking suspicion that it would take a while to dismiss Andrea Cunningham from his mind....

Dear Reader,

Why not sit back and relax this summer with Silhouette Desire? As always, our six June Desire books feature strong heroes and spirited heroines who come together in a highly passionate, emotionally powerful and provocative read.

Anne McAllister kicks off June with a wonderful new MAN OF THE MONTH title, *The Stardust Cowboy*. Strong, silent Riley Stratton brings hope and love into the life of a single mother.

The fabulous miniseries FORTUNE'S CHILDREN: THE BRIDES concludes with *Undercover Groom* by Merline Lovelace, in which a sexy secret agent rescues an amnesiac runaway bride. And Silhouette Books has more Fortunes to come, starting this August with a new twelve-book continuity series, THE FORTUNES OF TEXAS.

Meanwhile, Alexandra Sellers continues her exotic SONS OF THE DESERT series with *Beloved Sheikh*, in which a to-die-for sheikh rescues an American beauty-in-jeopardy. *One Small Secret* by Meagan McKinney is a reunion romance with a surprise for a former summer flame. Popular Joan Elliott Pickart begins her new miniseries, THE BACHELOR BET, with *Taming Tall, Dark Brandon*. And there's a pretend marriage between an Alpha male hero and blue-blooded heroine in Suzanne Simms's *The Willful Wife*.

So hit the beach this summer with any of these sensuous Silhouette Desire titles…or take all six along!

Enjoy!

Joan Marlow Golan
Senior Editor, Silhouette Desire

Please address questions and book requests to:
Silhouette Reader Service
U.S.: 3010 Walden Ave., P.O. Box 1325, Buffalo, NY 14269
Canadian: P.O. Box 609, Fort Erie, Ont. L2A 5X3

TAMING TALL, DARK BRANDON
JOAN ELLIOTT PICKART

SILHOUETTE *Desire*®
Published by Silhouette Books
America's Publisher of Contemporary Romance

With special thanks
to Tara Gavin,
Editor Extraordinaire!

SILHOUETTE BOOKS

ISBN 0-373-76223-2

TAMING TALL, DARK BRANDON

Copyright © 1999 by Joan Elliott Pickart

This edition published by arrangement with Harlequin Books S.A.

Look us up on-line at: http://www.romance.net

Printed in U.S.A.

JOAN ELLIOTT PICKART

is the author of over seventy novels. When she isn't writing, she enjoys watching football, knitting, reading, gardening and attending craft shows on the town square. Joan has three all-grown-up daughters and a fantastic little grandson. In September of 1995, Joan traveled to China to adopt her fourth daughter, Autumn. Joan and Autumn have settled into their cozy cottage in a charming small town in the high pine country of Arizona.

THE BACHELORS:

Brandon Hamilton:

Age 35. Hotel owner. 6 ft., nicely built. Black hair, dark eyes. Principled, protective…powerfully attractive.
TAMING TALL, DARK BRANDON,
June 1999, Silhouette Desire

Taylor Sinclair:

Age 36. Accountant. 6 ft., trim. Light brown hair, brown eyes. Self-confident, smart, stylish…sexy.
THE IRRESISTIBLE MR. SINCLAIR,
July 1999, Silhouette Special Edition

Ben Rizzoli:

Age 35. Doctor. 6 ft., rugged. Black hair, dark eyes. Private, precise, proud…purely potent.
THE MOST ELIGIBLE M.D.,
August 1999, Silhouette Special Edition

* * * *

These bachelor best friends have bet that marriage and family will never be part of their lives.

But they'll learn never *to bet against love.…*

Meet Brandon, Taylor and Ben
in bestselling author **Joan Elliott Pickart's**
engaging new miniseries

One

The sleek, candy-apple-red sports car hugged the curving mountain road as the powerful engine beneath the shiny hood won the challenge of the steep climb with ease.

Andrea Cunningham drove the vehicle at the exact speed limit, nodding in approval at the performance of her new possession.

The car was an early Christmas present to herself, an indulgence that had surprised even her when she'd purchased it two weeks before.

She'd been researching automobiles for well over six months, reading consumer reports, price comparing at various dealerships, and going for test drives in sedate, compact cars.

The only color she'd even considered had been white, due to the extreme heat in Phoenix. She'd wanted the best gas mileage, a proven history of easy maintenance, and ease of maneuverability in the congested, big-city traffic.

But she'd been in a strange, out-of-character mood the day she'd walked onto the new car lot and seen the gleaming red sports car that seemed to be calling her name.

An hour later, she had driven away in the catch-me-if-you-can red car.

Andrea flicked on the blinker, pressed on the gas pedal and whizzed past an eighteen-wheeler that was struggling to ascend the mountain. Safely in front of the big truck, she eased back into the right lane, then reduced her speed again to the exact number posted on the signs along the highway.

What on earth was she doing with a vehicle like this one? she thought, with a mental shake of her head. Granted, it had given her a bit of a rush to zoom past that big truck, knowing that if she was still driving her little compact car she'd be chugging slowly behind the eighteen-wheeler.

But this new car had cost her far more than she'd budgeted for when she finally admitted that her ten-year-old vehicle had to be replaced.

She, Andrea Cunningham, vice president of the firm of Challenge Advertising, was actually behind the wheel of a roaring, red sports car? It was unbelievable, ridiculous, and borderline embarrassing.

This car was not who she was, it was as simple as that.

Andrea sighed, her shoulders sagging a bit as a wave of fatigue swept through her, accompanied by the beginning of a throbbing headache.

She was furious at herself, at her body that hadn't kept up with the pace she'd been keeping at work.

The whole situation was so frustrating she could scream.

She'd been literally run out of town by her doctor, Andrea fumed. She'd finally gone in for a checkup, complaining of headaches, insomnia, lack of appetite, the inability to concentrate for great lengths of time and being so tired on occasion she'd been close to tears.

She was, the mighty medical man declared, suffering from complete physical exhaustion. He'd ordered her to take two full weeks off. No, she couldn't just cut back on her hours at the office, she was to get away, go somewhere peaceful and quiet, where her staff couldn't reach her. Only Jack, her boss, should be informed of her destination.

The doctor knew her personal history, was aware that she had no family to spend the holidays with. Her parents had been killed in an automobile accident when Andrea was only four.

There had been no loving relatives waiting in the wings to make a home for the frightened little girl, who had had her serene world shattered by the death of her mother and father.

She'd been raised in foster homes before she'd struck out on her own when she was eighteen.

Now she was heading to the small town of Prescott, where she'd never been before, and where her two-week sentence would include the Christmas holiday.

Being away from home on Christmas didn't matter. She paid little attention to the festive event. She gave gifts to a few close friends, but politely refused all invitations to Christmas dinner. It was a day for families, and Andrea had no desire to be odd-woman-out at anyone's table.

But being in Prescott for Christmas wasn't what had her hopping mad. It was the emotion of inadequacy, of not being up for all she'd taken on and promised to do. Complete physical exhaustion. That was infuriating.

The pain in Andrea's head increased, but she now knew the frequent headaches were caused by fatigue. They even had the official medical diagnosis of fatigue headaches.

She was only twenty-seven years old, for heaven's sake, not one hundred and seven. She was five foot six, weighed one hundred and twenty-two pounds, and had thought she was in tip-top shape.

Ha! What a joke. She was falling apart. A total wreck. Talk about embarrassing. This whole situation was mortifying.

What was she supposed to do in dinky little Prescott for two weeks? Sit in a rocking chair with a blanket over her knees and knit? She didn't know how to knit, and she certainly didn't know how to spend lazy days doing absolutely nothing.

She hated this. She really, really hated this.

Andrea was pulled from her fuming thoughts by the sudden slowing of traffic and the realization that she was approaching Prescott.

Glancing quickly at the piece of paper she had taped to the center console, she shifted into the left-hand lane. She'd written precise instructions to herself after carefully studying a map she'd spread out on her kitchen table.

An image of her empty apartment flitted in her mental vision, but it evoked no nostalgia or homesickness.

It was a group of rooms where she ate, slept and

spent very few leisurely hours, the majority of her life being centered on Challenge Advertising.

As her mind roamed from room to room in the high-rise apartment in Phoenix, she couldn't remember the last time she'd rearranged the furniture or purchased something new, pretty and personal for the place she'd called home for the past five years.

Why was she suddenly thinking about her dull apartment? she wondered. She'd do well to pay attention to her surroundings, or she'd probably drive right past Hamilton House, the hotel where she'd made reservations for the next two, long weeks.

"Oh, great," Andrea said aloud, frowning. "It's starting to snow. Isn't that just dandy?"

She hated cold weather. She hated snow. She hated Prescott, Arizona, and the reason that she was there.

Her doctor had suggested the small town, saying it was picture-perfect beautiful, with friendly people thrown in as an added bonus. Not having the time, nor the energy, to consider her options, she'd settled on Prescott without further thought.

"The crummy doctor might have mentioned that it snowed up here," Andrea said, stopping at a red light. "Oh-hh, I'm really hating this."

Brandon Hamilton stood behind the registration desk of Hamilton House, humming along with the carols that played softly in the large lobby of the hotel.

Excellent, he thought, looking down at a leather-bound registry. Once Ms. Andrea Cunningham arrived, Hamilton House would be booked solid through Christmas.

He couldn't ask for better than that, especially since

this was the first Christmas that he'd had the hotel up and running after the extensive renovations he'd put the charming old building through.

Brandon swept his gaze over the lobby, unable to curb the smile that formed on his lips.

Lookin' good, he thought. The huge, decorated Christmas tree in the front window was spectacular, and the gleaming, baby grand in front of it sat ready to be played.

Three separate groupings of high-backed, Victorian-era easy chairs surrounded low, round tables. The carpeting was authentic, cabbage roses on a black background, worn in spots but holding its own, considering that it had been on the floor since the turn of the century.

It was all paying off, he thought with a nod of satisfaction. The months of stress, of sleepless, worry-filled nights, of spending nearly every penny he had, plus the funds from a hefty loan from the bank, to restore Hamilton House to the majestic hotel it had been, had definitely been worth it.

Now all he needed was for Andrea Cunningham to show up and take possession of her room to give him that final emotional rush of knowing that the hotel was filled to the brim with happy guests.

Brandon glanced at his watch.

Two fifty-two, he thought. Check-in time was three o'clock. Where are you, Ms. Cunningham? He glanced at the front door, anticipating the sight of her smiling, ready-for-the-holidays face. Any moment now she would enter the hotel, filled with Christmas cheer.

Andrea got out of her car in the designated parking lot across from the hotel. She read the sign mounted on a post and frowned.

According to the instructions, she was to leave her luggage in her vehicle, if she chose to do so, and a member of the staff of Hamilton House would deliver it safely to her room.

Not a chance, she thought, glaring up at the large flakes of falling snow for a second. She was not about to announce, for all to hear, the description of her flashy car. She was having enough trouble adjusting to the fact that she actually owned the silly thing, without telegraphing the news to the world.

A few minutes later Andrea began her trek out of the parking lot, tilting slightly to one side due to the weight of her heavy suitcase.

The wet snow was sticking to the ground, causing her to slip and slide on her two-inch heels. The snow was also soaking the dark blue business suit that she wore with a pale blue silk blouse.

She didn't own a heavy coat, had no use for one in Phoenix. In her exhausted mental state, it just hadn't occurred to her to investigate the possible difference in weather between the valley and this mountain town.

Prescott was only a hundred miles away, for heaven's sake. That it was perched over five thousand feet up on a mountain was information she hadn't known until she had been well under way to arrive here.

It wasn't like her to be so disorganized, she thought, struggling to keep her footing as she crossed the street. But then, nothing about her life was in its proper order at the moment.

Andrea shuffled along the snowy sidewalk, shivering as she headed for the front door of the hotel, the suitcase feeling heavier with every treacherous step.

Her dark brown hair, which she kept in a blunt cut to just above her shoulders, was plastered to her head, creating icy-cold rivulets of water that dribbled inside her blouse collar and down her back.

She struggled with the stained-glass double doors to the hotel, pushed her slippery suitcase inside the building, then skidded in behind it, nearly toppling over the large piece of luggage.

She'd made it, she thought, and she could easily think of ten other places she'd rather be.

Brandon looked toward the front doors as the copper bell overhead tinkled that they had been opened. He did a double take as the incredible sight before him registered in his mind.

A woman, who was definitely teetering on her feet, was soaking wet and dotted with snowflakes. Her hair was streaming water, her suit appeared glued to her body, and she was *not* smiling with holiday cheer.

He had a sinking feeling in the pit of his stomach that this very wet and obviously freezing cold woman, who was becoming more furious with every passing second, was Ms. Andrea Cunningham.

"Oh, hell," Brandon muttered.

He rushed from behind the registration desk and across the lobby, then came to an abrupt halt in front of the woman, frantically searching his mind for something brilliant to say.

"Ms. Cunningham?" he said, beaming. "I'm Brandon Hamilton. Welcome to Hamilton House."

Before attempting to respond to the syrupy-sweet

greeting, Andrea took a deep, much-needed breath, then another, then one more. As she exhaled for the third time, a strange buzzing noise hummed in her ears and black dots paraded in front of her eyes.

She looked up into the dark eyes of Brandon Hamilton, blinked, then without having managed to speak one word...she fainted.

"Oh, Lord," Brandon said, his eyes widening.

As the woman he assumed was Andrea Cunningham began to crumple forward, Brandon's arms shot out instinctively. He scooped her up before she reached the highly polished tile floor of the entryway.

Brandon stood perfectly still for a moment, staring at the soggy bundle now nestled in his arms.

If this really was Andrea Cunningham, he thought, she was lovely, absolutely beautiful, in a wholesome way. Her eyes, which were now closed, were big and dark, her features were delicate, and her lips were made for kissing.

She was as light as a feather, even with soaking-wet clothes. She was fairly tall, maybe five-six, but she was exactly right for his six-foot frame.

How old was she? Maybe twenty-six or twenty-seven. The only thing that marred her pretty face were purple smudges of fatigue, or illness, beneath her eyes. She was—

"Cripe, Hamilton," he said aloud, snapping back to attention. "Don't just stand here. Do something."

He turned and saw the dining room hostess crossing the lobby.

"Jennifer," he called. "I need help."

The attractive woman hurried to where Brandon stood.

"My gosh, Brandon," she said. "What happened? Who is that? What's wrong with her?"

"I think she's our guest, Andrea Cunningham," he said. "Please get on the phone and call Ben Rizzoli. Tell him we need a doctor over here…quick. Then have Mickey take that suitcase behind the counter, and find someone to cover the front desk."

"Got it," Jennifer said, then hurried away.

Andrea stirred in Brandon's arms as he strode across the lobby and into his office. He kicked the door closed behind him and settled his precious cargo on a soft, beige leather sofa that was placed against one wall.

"Hello?" he said, hunkering next to the sofa. "Ms. Cunningham? Andrea?"

My, my, Andrea thought foggily, what a marvelously masculine voice that was calling her name. She was in the middle of the nicest dream, featuring one of the most ruggedly good-looking men she'd ever seen. He was "tall, dark and handsome" personified. The kind of man who appeared only in dreams or on the movie screen, but never walked around loose in real life.

He was holding her in strong arms against his rock-hard chest. He had broad shoulders, thick dark hair, and eyes so dark they appeared obsidian.

The timbre of his voice was perfect; deep, rich and rumbly. He'd said his name. Oh, what was it? Brandon. Yes, that was it. It suited him.

"Andrea?" Brandon said. "Can you hear me? Open your eyes. Please?"

Her name had never sounded so lovely, so feminine, Andrea thought. Brandon's voice floated over her, caressing her like plush velvet.

Oh, my, yes, this was a fantastic dream. But like all dreams, it had to end. She had to get up, go to work. She had so much that was waiting for her attention at the office.

Besides, she was terribly cold, chilled to the bone, in fact. The blankets on her bed felt clammy, as though she'd forgotten to put them in the dryer after removing them from the washing machine.

She wouldn't have made up her bed with wet linens, would she? No, of course not. Handsome man named Brandon or not, she'd had enough of this.

Andrea's lashes fluttered, then she opened her eyes slowly, taking a steadying breath in the process. In the next instant she gasped as she found herself staring at obsidian-eyed Brandon, the man from her dream.

"What are you doing here?" she said, attempting to sit up. "Don't you know the rules about dreams? I'm awake now, so get out of my bedroom."

"Easy, easy," Brandon said, pressing gently on her shoulders to keep her prone. "Are you Ms. Andrea Cunningham?"

"Yes, I am, but—"

"I'm Brandon Hamilton. Do you know where you are?" he said. Was she beautiful, but nuttier than a fruitcake? Rules about dreams? She thought she was in her own bedroom? "Just think for a second."

"You're Brandon?" Andrea said, frowning. "This doesn't make sense. The man in my dream said his name was—" Her eyes widened in horror. "Oh, my gracious, it wasn't a dream. I'm in Prescott. This is Hamilton House, and—"

"And you fainted right after you arrived," Brandon finished for her.

Cancel nuts, he thought. Andrea was hitting on all cylinders and was none too pleased with her reality. He had to keep her calm before she became hysterical or did something else that would disturb the tranquility of the hotel.

"There's a doctor on the way to see you," he said. "Everything is under control, Ms. Cunningham. Andrea. May I call you Andrea? We're not exactly strangers, you know. You fainted right into my arms, just like in the movies."

"I don't believe this," Andrea said, pressing one hand to her forehead. "I've never fainted in my life. I'm mortified, absolutely mortified. I'm going home."

"No, no," Brandon said quickly. "There's no need to be embarrassed." He produced his best hundred-watt smile. "You can't leave. You're my lucky charm—the guest who filled Hamilton House to capacity for the holidays. Lucky charms have responsibilities, you know."

"That," Andrea said, glaring at him, "is some of the corniest bunch of malarkey I've ever heard."

Brandon's smile slid off his chin. "Oh." He paused. "I have to admit, you scared the socks off me by fainting the way you did. I've never had *that* experience before here at Hamilton House."

Andrea closed her eyes for a moment, then looked at Brandon again.

"It's a first for me, too," she said.

A woman could drown in the depths of those fathomless dark eyes, she thought. A strange heat, which was far greater than the cold consuming her, was beginning to pulse low in her body. There was a blatant, masculine sexuality emanating from Brandon that was nearly overwhelming in its intensity.

"No one faints without a reason," Brandon said, pulling Andrea from her sensuous thoughts. "Maybe I should take you to the hospital if you're...well, if you're pregnant and something is definitely not as it should be."

"No," Andrea said, then sighed. "I'm not pregnant. I have no dread disease, nor mysterious ailment. I'm just tired."

"*Very* tired, then," Brandon said. "Let me guess. Your doctor has ordered you to rest, so you came up to Prescott from Phoenix."

"How did you know I'm from—oh, my registration information. I gave you my address."

Brandon nodded. "Where's your coat?"

"I don't own a heavy winter coat. I didn't investigate the weather up here. My doctor suggested Prescott and I came. This trip was *not* a good idea."

"Sure it was," Brandon said, smiling. "Prescott is a great place to get away from the rat race in Phoenix. What do you do for a living down in the valley?"

"I'm the vice president of Challenge Advertising."

And she was also a beautiful woman, Brandon thought. Was there a special man in Phoenix, who would be extremely distressed to learn that his lady had fainted into the arms of a complete stranger?

Well, if there was a guy, where was he when Andrea needed him, the louse? Forget the jerk. He, Brandon Hamilton, had been right on the spot to scoop Andrea into his arms. And, oh, man, how fantastic she'd felt nestled against him.

"Advertising." Brandon cleared his throat as a bolt of heat rocketed through his body at the remembrance of holding Andrea in his arms. "That's heavy stuff. Competitive. Pretty stressful, I imagine."

Andrea lifted her chin. "I enjoy my work and I'm very good at what I do."

"I don't doubt that for a minute, but you've apparently *enjoyed* your occupation right into total exhaustion. That, combined with suddenly being at a much higher altitude than you're accustomed to, is probably what caused you to faint.

"Your body is talking to you, Andrea, sending signals loud and clear. I've been down that road, and I suggest you listen to the message you're getting from yourself."

"Mmm," she said, frowning.

"You're registered to stay at Hamilton House for two weeks, so sit back and enjoy them."

"Right," she said, rolling her eyes heavenward. "I won't have to worry about being exhausted. I will die of boredom."

Brandon chuckled. "No, you won't. Prescott has a lot to offer. I'm a single man and I find plenty to do, and the people are warm and friendly."

"Who are you?" she said. "A representative for the chamber of commerce?"

Brandon shrugged. "Just stating the facts, ma'am." He paused. "I'm glad there's nothing seriously wrong with you, Andrea," he went on, looking directly into her eyes.

"Thank you," she said softly.

The seconds ticked by and neither moved nor hardly breathed as they continued to gaze into each other's eyes. A swirling heat seemed to weave around and through them, pulling them closer together, closer and closer....

A brisk knock sounded at the door, causing both

Andrea and Brandon to jerk in surprise at the sudden noise. A man entered the room in the next instant.

"Rizzoli to the rescue," he said cheerfully, crossing the room to stand by the sofa.

My stars, Andrea thought. Prescott, Arizona, had cornered the market on handsome men. This one was obviously Italian, indicated by his name and olive-toned skin. He, too, was tall, dark and handsome, his rough-hewed features boasting a nose that had obviously been broken at some point in his apparent thirty-odd years.

There was a subtle difference between the men, though. Brandon Hamilton was wearing what was obviously a custom-tailored suit. He had an aura of class and money, and his features were a tad more refined, smooth.

She would consider Mr. Rizzoli a diamond in the rough, in his faded jeans, plaid flannel shirt and fleece-lined, tan bomber jacket. His dark hair was also badly in need of a trim.

But they were a dynamic duo. Talk about mortifying. She now had two handsome men gawking at her. She wanted to crawl into a very deep hole and never come out.

"I'm definitely going home," she said, starting to sit up again.

"Whoa," Ben Rizzoli said, raising one hand. "I haven't done my rescue bit yet. I'm Dr. Benjamin Rizzoli, at your service. Call me Ben. Doctors have a terrible need to be needed, so you have to allow me to check you over or I'll pout. And you are?"

"Leaving," Andrea said again.

"She's Ms. Andrea Cunningham," Brandon told Ben. "She walked in the front door and fainted.

There's nothing wrong with her that a good rest won't cure. A rest she will definitely get by staying two weeks here at Hamilton House.''

Ben nodded. ''Well, Andrea—I'll call you Andrea and you call me Ben. We're very laid-back, friendly folks here in Prescott. I already know a great deal about you.''

''Do tell,'' Andrea said dryly.

''Okay, I will,'' he said, grinning. ''You're very organized and efficient. I mean, hey, you might have fainted before you came into the hotel and clunked your head on the snowy sidewalk. The fact that you waited to blink out after you entered this fine establishment proves my point. As for the rest of the diagnosis, it sounds as though Brandon has been doing my job for me. You're majorly tuckered out.''

''There you go,'' Brandon said, smiling.

''Do you two practice this routine?'' Andrea said, glowering at the pair. ''This is ridiculous. I'm going home.''

''Let's get serious here,'' Ben said, his expression now matching his statement. ''As a doctor, I have a few more questions for you, Andrea. Brandon, hit the road. I want to talk to Andrea alone.''

Brandon planted his hands on his thighs and pushed himself up to stand eye-to-eye with Ben.

''I'll be right outside the door,'' Brandon said. ''Holler if you need me.''

''Yep,'' Ben said. ''Go away.''

Brandon hesitated, looking at Andrea for a long moment, then left the room. He closed the door behind him and immediately began to pace back and forth in front of it.

What other questions did Ben want to ask Andrea?

he thought. Did Ben suspect there *was* something seriously wrong with her? No. No way. That was not acceptable.

Andrea. Pretty name. Pretty lady.

She had felt just so…so right in his arms, as though she belonged there, close to him, protected and cared for by him.

"Hell, Hamilton," he muttered. "Where is your mind going? You're sounding like the fruitcake you thought Andrea was."

But there was no denying the feelings of protectiveness and possessiveness he'd registered as he scooped Andrea into his arms and carried her into his office. She was so delicate, had become so pale, which had only accentuated the dark smudges beneath her eyes.

Brandon halted his trek and stared at the door.

Come on, Rizzoli, he mentally ordered. What in the hell was going on in there? He didn't want a major problem to have caused Andrea to faint.

No, she was fine, just fine. She had to be.

Brandon frowned and dragged one hand through his hair.

He was overreacting. Big-time. He didn't even know Andrea Cunningham. The cold fist of fear in his gut that she might be seriously ill didn't make one bit of sense, nor did the desire for her that had exploded throughout him.

Well, yes, maybe it did. He was a decent man, a nice human being. It wasn't Andrea, the woman, he was tied up in knots over, it was simply one person hoping that another person was all right. And it was simply a normal, healthy man's libido reacting to an attractive woman.

Anyone would feel as he did.

Wouldn't they?

Two

_____

Before Brandon could give further thought to the troubling, confusion-induced question in his mind, the door to the office opened and Andrea appeared, with Ben right behind her.

"Are you all right?" Brandon said, staring at Andrea intently. He switched his scrutiny to Ben. "Is she all right? You both look so serious. What's wrong? Why aren't you talking to me?"

Ben laughed. "You're using up all the air space, Hamilton. I've never seen you so rattled, which is very interesting, but how are we supposed to get a word in edgewise here?"

"Oh," Brandon said. "Sorry." He paused. "So? Say something, Rizzoli."

"I can't. There's such a thing as doctor-patient confidentiality, you know. If Andrea wishes to inform you that she is suffering only from complete exhaustion, combined with a dose of Prescott's altitude, that's up to her. My lips are sealed.''

"Oh, good grief," Andrea said, laughing. "You two are trouble, you really are."

"That's the first time you've smiled," Brandon said quietly, his gaze riveted on Andrea's face. "Your laughter reminds me of the sound of wind chimes."

"Well, I... Well..." Andrea started then stopped speaking as she looked directly into the depths of Brandon's dark eyes.

Those eyes again, she thought. They were pinning her in place. She couldn't move, or think, could hardly breathe. Brandon Hamilton had the most compelling, mesmerizing eyes she'd ever seen.

She wasn't freezing cold anymore. No, she was suffused with warmth, with steadily increasing heat that was thrumming low in her body and spreading rapidly throughout her.

Dear heaven, what was this man doing to her?

Ben cleared his throat.

"I hate to interrupt," he said, merriment dancing in his eyes. "But Andrea needs to get into some dry clothes and to eat something. My prescription is that you, Brandon, as the owner of Hamilton House, extend some extra tender loving care toward this weary guest. I definitely have the feeling that you can handle that."

"What?" Brandon said. "Oh, right. Sure thing. Yes. You bet."

"You're so articulate," Ben said, chuckling. "Well, I've got to get back to my office. I have patients waiting to—hey now, here are my favorite girlfriends."

Andrea's eyes widened as she saw two women,

who appeared to be in their seventies, bustling toward them.

The women were identical in size and features—mirror images of each other. But there the similarity stopped.

One was wearing a sedate gray, long-sleeved dress with a high, old-fashioned collar. The other was adorned in a flashy red satin number that reminded Andrea of pictures she'd seen of turn-of-the-century saloon girls.

The women smiled as they arrived where Andrea, Brandon and Ben were standing.

"Andrea," Brandon said, "may I present my great-aunts Prudence—" he swept one hand toward the woman in gray "—and Charity. The Hamilton twins."

"Hello," Andrea said, smiling.

"Good day, dear," Prudence said. "We heard you had the vapors, and thought perhaps we might be of assistance."

"Why would she want our help, Pru," Charity said, "when she has two hunks of stuff like Brandon and Ben fussing over her? All that's missing here is Taylor, our other handsome bachelor-on-the-loose."

"To know 'em is to love 'em, Andrea," Ben said. He kissed each of the elderly ladies on the cheek. "I'm gone. I'll check in with you later, Brandon."

"Goodbye, Benjamin," Prudence said.

"See ya, hotshot," Charity said.

Ben laughed as he strode away.

"Andrea needs to get settled into her room," Brandon said.

"It was a pleasure to meet you both," Andrea said to the women.

"Oh, you'll be seeing us again," Prudence said. "We live here in Hamilton House. How long will you be with us, dear?"

"Two weeks," Brandon said. "Come on, Andrea. We're not following Ben's orders by standing here. You need dry clothes and some food."

"Two weeks?" Charity said. "Don't you have a family that will miss you over the holidays?"

"Charity," Prudence said, "that is none of our business. You're being terribly nosy."

"Well, how am I supposed to find out what I want to know if I don't ask?" Charity said. "Andrea?"

"No," she said quietly. "I don't have any family, Miss Hamilton."

"Well, you do while you're here," Prudence said. "You call me Aunt Pru, dear, and Charity will be your Aunt Charity, and Brandon will be...well, just Brandon."

"He'll see to it that he's more than just Brandon if he has half the sense he claims to have," Charity said.

"Charity, hush," Pru said. "Mind your manners. You're being naughty."

Brandon gripped one of Andrea's arms and propelled her forward at a rapid pace.

"'Bye," she said over her shoulder to the aunts.

"Ta-ta, dear," Aunt Pru said.

"Put some makeup on," Aunt Charity said. "You're as pale as the ghosts who live in this place."

"Ghosts?" Andrea said.

"Ignore that," Brandon said.

At the registration desk, he released Andrea's arm and moved behind the counter.

"I'm sorry about my aunts," he said. "They can be a bit much at times."

"They're darling," she said, smiling. "For being twins, they certainly have different personalities."

"No joke. Forget what Aunt Charity said about ghosts. She just likes to keep things stirred up. Both Aunt Pru and Aunt Charity have hearts of gold, though."

"And you love them."

"Well, I... Yes. Yes, I love them very much."

Their eyes met across the gleaming counter that separated them.

Oh, Lord, Brandon thought, there it was again...the heat, that coiling heat, tight and low in his body. Andrea's great big dark eyes did unnerving things to his mind and, heaven help him, his libido.

"Sign this," he said, tearing his gaze from Andrea's. He shoved a card toward her. "I'll have Mickey show you to your room, and carry your suitcase for you. Would you like some hot soup and a sandwich sent up?"

"Yes, thank you, that would be lovely." Andrea paused. "Brandon, I apologize for all the trouble I've caused since I arrived."

"Don't give it another thought. You haven't been one bit of trouble."

No, the *trouble* stemmed from the strange and unsettling impact that Ms. Cunningham had on him. All she had to do was gaze at him with those big, expressive dark eyes of hers and he was consumed by a flash of heated desire.

Emotions he was very unaccustomed to were not doing anything for his peace of mind, either. That protectiveness and possessiveness he'd felt toward Andrea had come out of left field.

Oh, Andrea Cunningham was trouble, all right. He was going to have to keep his distance from the enchanting Andrea during her stay at Hamilton House.

He had an etched-in-stone rule about never becoming involved with a guest in the hotel. Not only was it tacky from a business angle, it was also potential heartache. Patrons checked in, then checked out. Poof. They were gone.

Jennifer came rushing to where Brandon stood behind the registration counter.

"I'm sorry, Brandon," she said breathlessly. "I was covering the desk, but got called to the dining room to solve a seating problem."

"Where's Teddy?" Brandon said.

"He went home with the flu. He was fine one minute, a sick puppy the next." Jennifer looked at Andrea and smiled. "I hope you're feeling better, Ms. Cunningham."

"It's Andrea, and I'm fine. Thank you."

"Wonderful," Jennifer said. "That means you'll be able to enjoy your stay at the hotel and take part in all the Christmas activities in Prescott. You picked the perfect place to be for the holidays. Oh, I'm Jennifer Mackane, the dining room hostess."

"She's more than that," Brandon said, smiling warmly at Jennifer. "She keeps that dining room running like a well-oiled machine. I'd be lost without her."

"How...admirable," Andrea said, smiling politely.

Jennifer Mackane was also beautiful, she thought, with a tumble of wavy, strawberry-blond hair that fell in fetching disarray to just above her shoulders, and pretty, sparkling green eyes.

She was tall, with a Barbie doll perfect figure, accentuated by a green wool holiday dress that had a stylish drape to it.

Brandon would be lost without her? Did he mean that literally? Was this the woman of importance in Brandon Hamilton's life?

Oh, for Pete's sake, Andrea, she admonished herself. What difference does it make? Who Brandon might, or might not, be romantically involved with was none of her business, nor did she care one iota.

She was simply having a typical feminine reaction to Jennifer Mackane. The hostess was stunning, while there *she* stood looking like a drowned mouse who had staggered in from the snow.

Enough of this nonsense.

"I really would like to go to my room and get settled in," Andrea said.

"Oh, yes, of course," Brandon said. "I'll page Mickey right now. He's our teenage jack-of-all-trades, Andrea."

"Mickey is across the street in the parking lot changing a tire for one of the guests," Jennifer said. "I'll cover the desk, Brandon. You can take Andrea upstairs."

Damn it, Brandon thought. He didn't want to. He'd just vowed to keep his distance from the woman. Seeing her to her room certainly wasn't following his own rule. Well, there was nothing he could do about it.

He retrieved the key packet from a drawer, picked up Andrea's suitcase and rounded the registration desk.

"Shall we go?" he said, looking anywhere but at Andrea.

"Gladly," Andrea said. "I'm already envisioning a hot shower, shampooing my hair, and putting on lusciously dry clothes."

Don't think about Andrea standing naked in the shower, Hamilton, he told himself, stifling a groan. The warm water would cascade over her delicate body, then she'd raise her arms in an oh-so-feminine gesture to shampoo her hair.

She might close her eyes in ecstasy at becoming warmed through after being so cold. She'd sigh, a womanly sigh of pleasure and—

"Come on," he said gruffly, starting across the large lobby.

"Gracious," Andrea said, hurrying to keep up with him.

Jennifer propped her elbow on the counter, cupped her chin in her hand and watched the pair heading for the elevator.

"Interesting," she said, smiling. "Very, very interesting."

Hamilton House was five stories high, and part of Brandon's restoration plan had been to create Victorian-era rooms, each with a slightly different decor. It had taken a seemingly endless number of hours conferring with a decorator to accomplish the feat, but Brandon was immensely pleased with the results.

Brandon's suite of rooms were on the fifth floor, as were the ones where Aunt Pru and Aunt Charity resided. Walls had been knocked down to create the two apartments, leaving only two rooms for guests. Andrea had been booked into one of those rooms.

After a silent ride in the elevator, Andrea smiled in delight when she finally entered her room. She swept her gaze over the charming area.

There was a dark wood, queen-size sleigh bed, a matching desk and dresser, a small round table with a chair, and an overstuffed easy chair. The walls were decorated in pale green and vanilla-striped wallpaper, with the bedspread a shade darker green. The plush carpeting was a lovely salmon color.

"Oh, this is beautiful," she said, turning to face Brandon where he stood just inside the closed door.

"I'm glad you like it." He placed her suitcase on a wooden luggage rack by the door, then put the key packet on top. "I'll have your food sent up in about an hour. Will that give you enough time to take your shower and...to do all that you are going to do?"

"Yes, thank you."

"Fine. Just call down to the desk if there's anything you need, want, whatever. Goodbye. Oh, welcome to Hamilton House. Forget that. I think I've said it to you about fifteen times already."

"Brandon?" Andrea said, frowning slightly. "Is something wrong? You seem to be...I don't know...angry all of a sudden."

Brandon took a deep breath, then exhaled slowly, puffing out his cheeks in the process.

"No, I'm not angry, Andrea," he said quietly. "I realize that I'm not behaving properly in my role as owner of Hamilton House. I'm sorry."

"It must be difficult," she said thoughtfully, "to have to always be *on*."

"I've been doing it for six months, ever since the renovations were completed and we had the grand

opening. This is the first time I've let my profession-
alism slip.''

Brandon shook his head.

"You have a strange effect on me, Ms. Cunningham. You're a spell-weaver. I look at you and I…
You've felt it, too, haven't you? The pull?''

Andrea wrapped her hands around her elbows.
"Yes," she whispered.

"We have to ignore it, to pretend it isn't there. You
realize that, don't you?''

"Of course I do," she said angrily. "You're speaking to me as though I'm an adolescent with uncon-
trollable hormones. I'm not a child, Brandon Hamilton. I'm a woman.''

"Believe me," he said, a weary quality to his
voice, "I'm very aware of that.''

"This…this whatever it is that has taken place between us is very understandable.''

"It is?" he said, crossing his arms over his chest.
"This ought to be good. Why don't you explain it to
me, since you have it all figured out.''

"Certainly," she said, lifting her chin. "In my
case, my overreaction reaction—''

"'Overreaction reaction'?" Brandon interrupted
with a burst of laughter.

"Do you mind?" she said with an indignant little
sniff. "I have the floor.''

"I humbly apologize," he said, curbing his smile.
"You were saying?''

"Yes. Well, my *ridiculous* reaction to your…
masculinity is due to the fact that I am in a state of
total exhaustion. I'm a tad vulnerable, not conducting
myself as I normally would.''

"I see," Brandon said, stroking his chin. "That makes sense, I guess."

"Indeed it does. Granted, you're a very attractive man, but I deal with good-looking men every day in my profession. They don't cause me to be unable to think, make it impossible for me to move, or breathe, when they look at me."

"But *I* do?" he said, grinning again.

"Would you stop it?" she said, planting her hands on her hips.

Brandon cleared his throat. "Sorry."

"Once I've rested," Andrea continued, "I'll be fine. No problem. You'll just be another handsome man in a long line of same who cross my path and whom I ignore."

Brandon narrowed his eyes. "Is that a fact?"

"It is," she said with a decisive nod.

"And *my* overreaction reaction to *you?* Would you care to explain that, as well?"

"It's very simple, Brandon. Fainting in your arms brought out the Tarzan-Jane, knight-in-shining-armor instinct in you. It's nothing to get all in a dither about."

"Let me be certain I have this straight," Brandon said. "I'm suffering from a massive machismo rush because you fainted?"

"Yes."

"And you'll view me as just another man in the multitude of men out there once you've overcome your state of exhaustion?" Brandon started toward her slowly. "Have I got that right?"

"Well, I guess... Well, yes, that about sums it up," Andrea said, taking a step backward as Brandon continued to advance.

A shiver coursed through Andrea. Was this fear? she thought frantically. Brandon seemed suddenly like a sleek panther stalking his prey—her. Was she frightened? No, it was a strange, sensual *excitement* that was consuming her, causing that thrumming heat to pulse low in her body once again.

This was insane! She should stand her ground, demand that Brandon Hamilton leave her room immediately. Yes, that was exactly what she should do.

But she wasn't going to.

Because a part of her that she hadn't even realized existed wanted to know, had to find out, just exactly what Brandon intended to do when he finally closed the distance between them.

Brandon stopped in front of Andrea and cradled her face in his large hands. He looked directly into her dark eyes, and his voice was deep and rumbly, and very, very male when he spoke.

"Your grand theories may be on the mark for all I know," he said. "I really don't have a clue. What I *do* know is that I resent being heaped with every other guy in a pair of pants. That's totally unacceptable."

"I certainly didn't intend to insult you," Andrea said, her voice trembling slightly. "I was just explaining my theory about what's happening between us."

"Mmm. Well, put this in your data bank, Ms. Cunningham, and see if you don't come up with a rather different conclusion."

Oh, my gosh, Andrea thought, he's going to kiss me. No!

Brandon lowered his head and captured Andrea's mouth in a searing kiss, parting her lips, delving his tongue inside the sweet darkness to seek and find her tongue.

Yes! Andrea thought, her lashes drifting down.

Their bodies were inches apart, not touching, yet the heat of rising passion wove around and through them, as though they were one entity.

The kiss went on and on, and desires soared.

What in the hell are you doing? a voice thundered in Brandon's head.

He was allowing his damnable male ego to run roughshod over common sense and decorum.

For Pete's sake, man, get a grip.

Brandon broke the kiss, took a ragged breath, and dropped his hands from Andrea's face. Without speaking, he turned and strode from the room, closing the door behind him with more force than was necessary.

Andrea blinked, placed one hand on her racing heart, then rested the fingertips of her other hand on her tingling lips.

Never in her entire life had she experienced a kiss like the one she'd just shared with Brandon.

That kiss had stolen the very breath from her depleted body.

That kiss had created vivid images in her mind of clothes being torn away so that there was no barrier between her and Brandon.

That kiss had been the prelude to slow, exquisite lovemaking with Brandon that would have been ecstasy in its purest form.

That kiss never should have taken place.

"The nerve of that arrogant man," she said, narrowing her gaze. "How dare he just march across the room and kiss me senseless? Just who in the blue blazes does he think he is?''

In the next instant she sighed, her shoulders slumping as fatigue swept over her.

She could rant and rave from here to Sunday, she thought dismally, but it wouldn't erase the fact that she had been a very willing partner in that kiss. She'd savored every sensuous, heart-stopping second of it, and had *not* wanted it to end.

She had never behaved so recklessly, so…so wantonly.

''I'm not myself,'' she said, pressing one hand to her forehead.

She didn't care how angry her theories had made Brandon. They were sound and true. Her state of exhaustion was causing her to act and react out of character.

She would dismiss from her mind what had taken place in that room with Brandon. When she saw him again in the hotel, she'd be pleasant but cool, nod a greeting, and keep moving. She would not engage in further conversation with Mr. Hamilton, and she certainly would never be alone with him again.

The rest she desperately needed would restore her to normal, she told herself. The two-week sentence she was facing in this freezing cold little town would pass quickly, then she'd get into her ridiculous red sports car and whiz back down the mountain to Phoenix, where she belonged.

With a decisive nod, Andrea retrieved her suitcase, opened it and removed dry clothing. When she entered the bathroom, she gasped as she saw her reflection in the mirror above the sink.

"Oh, good night," she said with a burst of laughter.

She looked like a drenched kitten. Her hair was sticking up in places and was plastered to her head in others. The circles beneath her eyes were darker than ever, making her appear ghostly. Her suit and blouse were wrinkled and soggy.

"Why on earth," she said, leaning closer to the mirror, "would a man like Brandon Hamilton want to kiss *you?*"

Andrea straightened and then frowned, aware of a funny chill tiptoeing around her heart.

Brandon hadn't wanted to kiss *her,* she thought. He would have kissed anyone who had insulted his masculine ego the way she had. The kiss had been a product of his anger, not his desire for her.

That made sense.

Then why, if that was so all-fired reasonable, was she registering feelings of disappointment and rejection?

"Oh, I don't know," she said, unbuttoning her suit jacket. "And I don't care. Just forget it."

Please, Andrea, she thought, dropping the sodden jacket to the floor, *just forget it. For your own good.*

Three

When Brandon left Andrea's room, he glanced longingly at his apartment door at the end of the hallway, then shook his head and went to the elevator. He hesitated, his finger poised at the button.

He'd walk down the five flights of stairs, he decided, in lieu of taking some much-needed private time in his apartment. It wouldn't be fair to Jennifer to leave her stranded at the front desk when she had things to tend to in the dining room.

Brandon started down the wide, carpeted stairway, each step thudding in an angry cadence directed at himself.

He should be shot at dawn, he mentally fumed. Strung up by the thumbs. Tarred and feathered. Run out of town on a rail.

Where was his brain? His sense of right and wrong? He was the proprietor of a hotel, who had blatantly kissed one of the guests without her permission. Cripe, he was probably staring at a lawsuit that would wipe him out financially. One kiss and he would now be rendered a moneyless derelict, living on the streets of Prescott.

Brandon stopped on the landing of the third floor and dragged both hands down his face.

Andrea Cunningham had pushed his macho buttons, and he'd behaved like a Neanderthal. For reasons he couldn't fathom, her dismissal of the fiery attraction between them had ignited his fury. He'd become blindly determined to prove her ridiculous theory wrong.

So, he'd kissed her.

With a shake of his head, Brandon resumed his plodding trek down the stairs.

That kiss, he mused, had been sensational. Desire, hot and heavy and coiling, had exploded within him like a rocket. He'd been consumed by it, and had come very close to losing total control.

Brandon narrowed his eyes.

That reaction, by damn, had been mutual. Andrea had returned the kiss in heated abandon.

What did that mean? Why hadn't she shoved him away, smacked him right across the face, then hollered the roof down?

Hell, he didn't know what had gone on in Andrea's mind when he'd kissed her, nor what she might be thinking now that she was alone. Women were so complicated, he wouldn't live long enough to understand any of them.

The question at hand was…now what?

What should he do, say, how should he act, the next time he saw Andrea?

Maybe he should just wait and see, take his cue from *her*. That seemed like a very good idea, since he was messing up royally when left to his own devices.

"You're such an idiot, Hamilton," he muttered as he reached the lobby.

Jennifer smiled at Brandon when he returned to the registration desk.

"Did you get Andrea all taken care of?" she said.

"In a manner of speaking," he said gruffly.

Jennifer frowned. "What does that mean?"

"Nothing. Would you have some soup and a sandwich sent up to Andrea in about an hour?"

"Yes, but—" Jennifer glanced at her watch "—it's getting late. Don't you think Andrea will be ready for a full dinner?"

"Good thought."

"Why don't you call her and ask if she'd like dinner sent up, or if she plans to come down to the dining room? For all we know, she might wish to leave the hotel for her meal. Yes, you'd best phone her, Brandon."

"No," he said quickly.

"Why not?"

"Because...because that's not efficient time management, Jennifer. I'd have to track you down if Andrea told me she'd like to eat in her room. Therefore, you call her."

"Well, all right." Jennifer paused. "Andrea's quite pretty, don't you think? Even not being at her best, she's attractive. She has lovely eyes."

"Mmm," he said, straightening some brochures that didn't need straightening.

"I hope she doesn't get lonely spending the holidays in a hotel. No family. No friends here. That sounds like a rather bleak Christmas.''

"It's none of our business, Jennifer. Don't you have something to do in the dining room?''

"Maybe we should invite Andrea to the staff Christmas party." Jennifer went on as though Brandon hadn't spoken. "That might brighten things up a bit for her.''

"Don't be silly. We can't start doing something like that. What if other guests hear that Andrea was included in the staff party? No, absolutely not. Staff is staff. Guests are guests.''

Except that he'd kissed the socks off the guest under discussion, Brandon thought. Hell.

"All right, Mr. Scrooge," Jennifer said. "Maybe the aunties will take Andrea under their wing so she won't be quite so lonely.''

"I'm sure they will. They're aware of the fact that Andrea doesn't have any family.''

"No family at all? No one?''

Brandon shrugged. "Apparently not.''

"That's sad, it really is. I wonder why an attractive woman like Andrea isn't married?''

"I'd say she's married to her work, because Ben said she was suffering from exhaustion.''

"Oh, I see," Jennifer said, nodding. "She needs to learn how to stop and smell the flowers.''

"Jennifer, do you realize you have me standing here gossiping about one of our guests? I don't do things like this. Go away.''

Jennifer laughed. "Yes, boss. Whatever you say, boss. Your wish is my command.''

"I should hope so.''

"You never did say if you agree with me that Andrea is pretty."

"Goodbye, Ms. Mackane," Brandon said, frowning at her. "Go earn your keep."

"'Bye," she said, wiggling the fingers of one hand at him.

"Women," Brandon mumbled as Jennifer disappeared from view.

The next two hours flew by as Brandon was approached time and again by guests with questions needing to be answered.

He supplied brochures listing the holiday activities taking place in Prescott, arranged for the mailing of Christmas gifts that had been purchased in town, helped several couples decipher maps for destinations of outings planned for the next day, and answered the telephone, telling three frantic, local hostesses that Hamilton House had no vacancies.

No vacancies, Brandon mentally repeated as he replaced the telephone receiver. That was due to the arrival of the woman who had taken occupancy of the last available room in the hotel.

Andrea.

Jennifer had appeared briefly an hour before to announce that Andrea had requested that a salad, small steak and a pot of tea be delivered to her room. Jennifer had looked at him intently, as though expecting a major reaction regarding Andrea's choices for dinner. He'd simply shrugged, causing Jennifer to glare at him and stomp away.

What had Jennifer wanted him to say about Andrea's meal, for Pete's sake? Food was food.

Now that he really thought about it, however, Andrea hadn't ordered very much to eat, which was probably the point Jennifer had been attempting to make. Andrea should have added a potato, vegetables and dessert to her dinner. She was physically exhausted, and should be consuming more food to bolster her energy.

When he'd held Andrea in his arms after she fainted, he'd been aware, very aware, of how delicate she was, how fragile. She needed someone to look after her, to take care of her.

Brandon shook his head and frowned.

Yeah, right, he thought dryly. Andrea was a big-city executive, who was dedicated to her career to the exclusion of everything else, including her own health and welfare.

She didn't want, nor seemed to need, anyone intruding on her focused life.

He'd lived that type of existence for more years than he cared to admit. When he'd suddenly suffered from chest pains, his doctor had told him that he was a lucky man. His body had warned him of a potential heart attack waiting in the wings even though he was only thirty-five years old. Brandon decided then to make some adjustments in his life-style.

So, he'd walked away from the world of high-pressure, corporate law in New York City, taken courses in hotel management, and returned to Prescott, to his roots, to take possession of Hamilton House and begin the restorations that were needed so badly.

The charming old building had been in the Hamilton family since the day it was built at the turn of the century. When his great-grandfather had died, the series of leases had begun, the hotel falling into good hands at times and into inefficient care at others.

When Brandon had stepped into the picture, poor old Hamilton House was a disaster, both physically and financially.

Granted, there had been extreme stress as he undertook the project, but his attitude was far different than it had been in New York. He was happy, content, and he'd viewed the challenge before him with enthusiasm. There had been no further chest pains.

A young couple strolled arm and arm across the lobby, catching Brandon's attention and pulling him from his thoughts.

He watched the couple head for the elevator, and hoped the bride and groom had enjoyed the fruit basket and champagne the hotel had sent up to their room to celebrate their wedding.

A strange chill swept through him as the couple stepped into the elevator and kissed as the doors swished closed.

What was *this* new emotion he was feeling? he thought crossly. Was it, possibly, just a tiny twinge of loneliness? The holiday season could evoke that emotion in a man who was alone, he supposed.

There had been an endless string of women in his jet-set life in New York. His idle hours back then had been filled with social activities, but he hadn't been in the private company of a woman since returning to Prescott.

Until now.

Until Andrea.

And he'd kissed her.

Brandon bit back an earthy expletive as the mere remembrance of their kiss caused the now familiar, coiling heat of desire to twist low and painfully in his body.

That woman was a menace. She did tricky little things to his mind and wreaked total havoc with his body. The two weeks that Andrea was scheduled to stay at the hotel couldn't pass quickly enough, as far as he was concerned.

Two weeks. Then Andrea would repack her suitcase, settle her bill, and leave. She'd be gone, never to be seen again.

Never? his mind echoed.

Well, sure. That was how it was with guests of the hotel. They came, they went, end of story. Unless Andrea decided to visit Prescott again at some point in the future, and stayed at Hamilton House while doing so, she'd be out of sight, out of mind forever, in two weeks.

Wrong, Brandon thought in the next instant. He had a sneaking suspicion that it would take a while to dismiss Andrea Cunningham from his mind totally.

Brandon glanced at the elevator door.

Would those newlyweds celebrate a fiftieth wedding anniversary? he wondered. Or would they be another divorce statistic? He'd known only two couples in his large social circle in New York who had been married for more than five years.

Marriage. He'd given fleeting thought to the institution once or twice in the past decade, then dismissed the idea as not being his cup of tea. He wasn't alone in his confirmed bachelor status. His best buddies, Ben and Taylor, had never expressed a yearning to marry, either. His own fast-lane existence in New York had had no room for hearth and home, wife and babies.

But now?

He was home. He was back in Prescott, where he'd grown up in a loving environment with parents who adored him. Parents who had been killed in a plane crash when he was a freshman in college. His family now consisted of Aunt Pru and Aunt Charity, and he was fortunate to have the dear old ladies in his life.

Marriage, Brandon's mind echoed.

Why was he suddenly dwelling on the subject? Well, because it was Christmas, a sentimental, family oriented holiday. It was the time of year, that was all, that was rendering him a bit vulnerable in the emotional department, making him acutely aware of his single status.

"Damn," he muttered, frowning.

He'd been slam-dunked by more confusing, powerful emotions today than he had in the past year. Ever since Andrea had staggered in the front doors of the hotel, he'd been off-kilter.

What he needed was to end this day and start fresh tomorrow. He'd be fine after a solid night's sleep. He would then be able to view Andrea as an attractive woman, who just happened to be staying at the hotel for two weeks. A guest. A here-today, gone-tomorrow person, like the multitude before her and those yet to come.

But that whole concept would be easier to believe if he hadn't kissed Andrea Cunningham.

"Good evening, dear," Aunt Pru said, bringing Brandon from his rambling thoughts.

"What?" he said. "Oh, hello, Aunt Pru. Aunt Charity. Did you enjoy your dinner?"

"Oh, my, yes," Aunt Pru said. "Very much so.

Are you partaking of your evening meal in the dining room tonight, dear?''

"No, I don't think so," Brandon said. "I'm not that hungry. I'll make myself a sandwich in my apartment. Jerry will be here to relieve me in a few minutes, then I'll head upstairs.''

"Jerry is a charming young man," Aunt Pru said. "These days, though, he's a bundle of nerves as he awaits the birth of his first child.''

"I don't know why he's all in a tizzy," Aunt Charity said. "He has done his part toward having that kid. The tough stuff is yet to come—and that will be accomplished by his wife. Then Jerry will puff himself up and take all the credit for producing an heir.''

"That's not quite fair, Charity," Prudence said. "Jerry is nervous because he loves his wife and unborn child. He wants this momentous event over, knowing all went well. That's a part of love and marriage.''

"Speaking of which…" Brandon said, striving for a casual tone of voice. "Do you two ever regret not marrying, or having a family?''

"Bite your tongue," Charity said. "I never intended to pick up some fool's dirty socks.''

Prudence sighed. "After my beau was killed in the war, I never found another who touched my heart. My dreams of a husband and children faded into oblivion. I'll be so pleased when *you* marry, Brandon, and bring a baby into our lives to pamper.''

"Won't happen," Charity said. "Brandon is a bedhopper.''

"I am not!" Brandon said, nearly yelling. He glanced around quickly, then lowered his voice. "That was a terrible thing to say, Aunt Charity.''

Charity shrugged. "Facts are facts. I don't see a wedding ring on your finger, big boy."

"Things are different these days," Prudence said. "Young people concentrate on their careers, not romance. That lovely Andrea is a perfect example of what I'm referring to. Even if Brandon came courting, I imagine Andrea would send him on his way."

"She might settle for a whing-ding of an affair first," Charity said.

"Charity, please," Prudence said. "You do upset my sensibilities at times. I do wish you'd think before you speak."

"What is there to think about?" Charity said. "Andrea wouldn't marry Brandon on a bet."

"Why not?" Brandon said. "What am I, chopped liver? I wouldn't be a bad catch, except for the fact that I'm in debt up to my eyebrows. But I'm kind, pleasant, intelligent."

"So is a cocker spaniel," Charity said. "What would Andrea need you for beyond the bedroom? She's a no-nonsense career woman, as far as I can tell."

She also kisses like a dream, Brandon thought. There was a sizzling, sensuous woman beneath the business suit that Andrea wore.

"Maybe," Prudence said, "Andrea yearns for a husband and family, but has buried those dreams because of her demanding career. That would be a shame. True love could pass her by without her realizing it, because she'd never see the butterflies dancing."

"The who?" Brandon said, frowning in confusion.

"The butterflies, dear." Prudence sighed wistfully. "Oh, how the beautiful butterflies danced when I was strolling in the garden with my beau, rest his soul. The butterflies know, you see, often before the couple themselves realize it, that true love is in bloom like a lovely flower. Then the butterflies dance, and it's a glorious sight to behold.''

Brandon laughed. ''Well, I guess with that theory, no one would fall in love in Prescott in the winter. There sure aren't any butterflies romping around in that snow out there.''

''You're wrong on that score, hotshot,'' Charity said. ''The butterflies would show up to dance their jig no matter what the season was.''

''*You* believe in this butterfly thing, Aunt Charity?'' Brandon said.

''I have to admit that I do,'' Charity said, nodding. ''Because I saw the butterflies dancing around Prudence and her beau in the garden all those years ago. Prudence's young man came home on leave from the war in the dead of winter, too, and the butterflies suddenly appeared, dancing up a storm.''

''Yes,'' Prudence said softly, staring into space. ''Yes, they did.''

''You know I chatter on about there being ghosts in Hamilton House, Brandon,'' Charity said. ''But that's nonsense, just something I blather about to tickle people's fancy. But the butterflies? They are real, they truly are. There's no denying it.''

''Oh,'' Brandon said, then for the life of him couldn't think of one other thing to say.

''It's so sad,'' Prudence said, ''when people are so busy, so caught up in their careers, that they don't see the butterflies, and miss out on the rapturous joy of true love. That's what I fear might happen with Andrea.''

"It could happen to you, too, big boy," Charity said to Brandon, "if you don't watch your step. Oh, I know you're supposedly a fast-lane dropout from New York City, but you haven't taken a day off since you arrived back in Prescott and took over the hotel."

"I've been rather busy, if you recall," Brandon said, running one hand down his tie. "This place didn't get shaped up on its own, you know."

"But now the restoration work is completed," Charity said. "And has been for months. It's time you played a bit, instead of doing nothing but working day and night. It's starting to seem as though you just changed the cities where you live, but not the life-style you lead."

Brandon planted his hands on the counter and leaned toward Charity.

"Are you forgetting that you sold your family house," he said quietly, "and invested that money in the hotel? Everything you had is tied up in this endeavor. I'd think you'd be relieved to see that I'm dedicated to making Hamilton House successful."

"The hotel is doing just fine," Charity said. "It's time for you to lighten up."

Brandon straightened and smoothed the lapels on his jacket.

"Yes, well, after the new year rolls in," he said, "things will calm down around here. In the meantime…" He shrugged.

"In the meantime," Prudence said, "*you* might miss seeing the butterflies dancing, dear." She paused. "Well, shall we go upstairs, Charity?"

"Ready for some gin rummy, Brandon?" Charity said. "Penny a point."

"No, thanks. Not tonight," he said. "It's been a

rather…hectic day. I'm looking forward to putting my feet up and relaxing."

"All right, dear," Prudence said. "We'll see you in the morning. Come along, Charity."

As Brandon watched the aunts cross the lobby and disappear into the elevator, he shook his head.

That conversation had been ridiculous from start to finish. Butterflies dancing when love was in bloom? Cripe.

What was next? Aunt Pru and Aunt Charity would announce that there really was a Santa Claus and Brandon should leave cookies and milk out for the fat guy in the red suit on Christmas Eve?

Oh, well, he loved Aunt Pru and Aunt Charity, even if they were nonsensical on occasion.

Brandon's attention was caught by the sound of music from the far side of the lobby. He exchanged a smile with the man now sitting at the baby grand in the glow of the tall, twinkling Christmas tree.

There you go, butterflies, Brandon thought. If they got wind that love was in bloom at Hamilton House, the hotel would even provide the music for their dance.

"Ridiculous," Brandon muttered.

In the next moment he squinted and swept his gaze over the entire lobby.

Oh, that cooks it, he thought. For a second there, he'd actually been making certain there weren't any butterflies.

He'd already determined that what he needed was for this unsettling day to end, so he could start fresh tomorrow after a good night's sleep. That was definitely on his agenda.

Would Andrea sleep well? he wondered. Would

she have accepted the fact that she was in Prescott for two weeks, like it or not, and be prepared to enjoy herself?

Hell, what he should be concerned about was whether the new day would restore his sense of control.

And if, at dawn's light, he would have forgotten…just pushed into a dusty corner of his mind, the exquisite kiss he'd shared with Andrea Cunningham.

Somehow, he thought dismally, he didn't think a night's sleep would accomplish that.

Four

The next morning, Andrea sat at a table in the charming dining room of the hotel, consuming a meal of tea, toast and a bowl of fresh fruit.

A map of Prescott was spread before her on the table, along with a brochure listing the stores in town and what they offered for sale.

Andrea took a sip of the hot, delicious tea, then glanced around the large, pretty room, full of people enjoying their breakfast. There was a hum of nearly palpable excitement in the air, and the noise level was high as everyone talked and laughed.

Holiday spirit, Andrea thought, sighing as she replaced the china cup on the saucer. Maybe she would soak some of it up by osmosis, be lifted out of her gloomy mood.

No, she wasn't exactly down in the dumps. It was

more a flat-line feeling, of being neither up nor down, just…there.

She'd slept soundly in the big, comfortable bed and had actually been a bit hungry when she'd awakened. She'd even managed to push the mortifying scene in her room with Brandon Hamilton to the back of her mind, refusing to dwell on it for one second longer.

She'd dressed in dark blue slacks, a bright red sweater and loafers. The Christmassy sweater, however, had not automatically propelled her into a festive frame of mind.

Well, that made sense, she mused. She'd never before been caught up in the hustle and bustle and crackling enthusiasm of the holidays. Why should this year be any different?

It was just that she wasn't usually surrounded by people at this time of year who were so *happy*. She felt out of place, like a misfit.

And for some reason, she didn't like that feeling, not one little bit.

Brandon stepped out of the elevator and crossed the lobby to the registration desk. He checked in with Ryan, the clerk on duty, was told that all was well, then headed for the dining room.

He was going out to play, he decided. He'd been unable to dismiss what Aunt Charity had scolded him about the night before, regarding not having taken a day off since returning to Prescott, and having done nothing to change his nose-to-the-grindstone work routine.

Aunt Charity was right. He'd kept up his grueling schedule at the hotel far longer than was necessary. Heart attacks hit men in laid-back little towns like

Prescott, just as they did in the chaos of New York City. Well, Brandon Hamilton was *not* going to join that rank and file.

Yes, sir, he was taking the entire day off. He'd leave the hotel and—

Brandon slowed his step and frowned.

And do what? Damn, it had been so long since he'd had any free time, he didn't have a clue how to fill his idle hours.

He'd accomplished his Christmas shopping in one evening by ordering gifts from catalogs for the aunts, Ben Rizzoli, Jennifer and Joey, Taylor Sinclair, and the staff of Hamilton House. A few envelopes, stamps and hefty checks, and that had been that.

The items had arrived by mail. He'd wrapped each with less-than-expertise technique and then stacked them on a closet shelf in his apartment, awaiting the big day. End of story.

Well, the guests of the hotel managed to keep busy while visiting Prescott, he thought, as he entered the dining room. He'd have some breakfast, then head out to see what he could find to occupy his time.

The problem was, he'd grown up here, and had seen all the unique offerings of the town a thousand times.

The assistant manager of the dining room greeted Brandon with a smile.

"Good morning, Brandon," the man said. "Nice crowd for breakfast."

"I can see that, Peter," Brandon said, matching the man's smile. "It won't hurt my feelings one bit if you don't have a table free for me."

Brandon swept his gaze over the room, pleased that the hotel's restaurant was once again proving to be a popular place to eat. His heart did a funny little two-step when he saw Andrea peering at a map where she sat at one of the tables. His smile faded.

There was Andrea Cunningham in the light of the new day.

The punch of sudden heat low in his body was definitely informing his brain that getting a good night's sleep had not diminished Ms. Cunningham's sensual impact on him one iota. Damn.

"I should have a free table in ten or fifteen minutes," Peter said. "If the folks don't linger over coffee."

"No, I have a plan," Brandon said, narrowing his gaze.

If he couldn't beat her, he thought, he'd join her. Yes, sir, that was the ticket. He'd go toe-to-toe with Andrea, and soon realize that she was just another attractive woman, not one to knock him for a loop. It was the circumstances of her arrival that had unsettled him, not the lady herself.

"You'll eat outside the hotel?" Peter said.

"What? Oh, no, I'll have breakfast here." Brandon grabbed one of the menus from the stack on the top of the podium that held the reservation book. "I'll be dining with one of our guests. Send a waitress over to the table, would you, please?"

"Sure thing."

Brandon made his way across the room, smiling and nodding at guests as he passed them, his resolve growing firmer with each step.

"Hello, Andrea," he said, stopping next to her chair. "Do you mind if I join you?"

Andrea's head snapped up and she stared at Brandon.

In a royal blue sweater and jeans, Brandon was just as devastatingly gorgeous as he'd been in a custom-tailored suit. She'd be *out* of her mind to allow him to join her at that table.

"Um…" she said.

"Thank you. You're most kind." Brandon pulled out the chair next to her, sat down and flipped open the menu. He gave it his full attention, even though he knew every item that was on it. "Hmm. What shall I have for breakfast this morning?"

Andrea looked sensational in red, he thought. That sweater made her lovely skin glow and those incredible big eyes seem even darker. She appeared somewhat rested, the smudges beneath her eyes not so prominent. Her hair was shining, and had swung like a silken curtain around her face when she'd raised her head.

It was a good thing he knew this menu by heart, he thought dryly, because he wasn't comprehending one thing he was supposedly reading.

So far, his plan was a dud, but it was early yet.

Brandon placed the menu to one side, crossed his arms on the top of the table and smiled at Andrea.

"Sleep well?" he said.

"Yes, thank you," she said stiffly. "I didn't allow *anything* to clutter my mind, and slept like a baby."

Score one for Ms. Cunningham, Brandon thought, forcing himself to keep his smile firmly in place. She was letting him know—about as subtly as whacking him on the head with a brick—that she hadn't given a moment's thought to the kiss they'd shared.

"I tossed and turned a bit," he said. "I had an issue of importance to mull over."

"Oh?" she said, feeling a shiver slither down her

back. Was Brandon saying that he'd lost sleep because of her? Because of the kiss they'd shared? Well, fancy that.

"Yep," he said. "My aunt Charity told me that I needed to take a day off, that I was working just as hard here as I had in New York City."

"Oh," Andrea said. No, darn it, that was *not* disappointment she was registering. It definitely was *not*. "I see."

"Aunt Charity was absolutely right," Brandon went on. "And the situation needs correcting immediately. So, I'm taking the day off, going out to play." He glanced at the map spread over the table. "It appears that you have big plans. Where are you headed?"

"Nowhere fancy," Andrea said, switching her gaze to the map. "I need to buy a coat. The trick is to figure out where to go, then how to get there without freezing to death."

Putty in his hands, Brandon thought smugly. Andrea was serving up the perfect opportunity for him to spend much-needed time in her company without having to scramble for an excuse to do so. This was going to be even easier than he ever imagined.

"No problem," Brandon said. "I'll take you shopping for a coat, and I'll warm up my vehicle before you leave the hotel."

"Oh, but…" Andrea started, only to be interrupted by a waitress appearing at the table.

"Hi, Brandon," she said. "Breakfast?"

"Yes, please. I'll have the Number Three." He looked at the dishes by Andrea. "You didn't have much to eat. Would you like some waffles?"

"No, this is plenty for me."

"Number Three coming right up," the waitress said, then hurried away.

"You really should eat more, Andrea," Brandon said. "Ben would tell you the same thing, I'm sure of it. You'll cure your exhaustion much quicker if you consume more fuel for the furnace, as the saying goes."

"Thank you, Dr. Hamilton," she said, frowning at him. "About shopping for my coat. I really don't—"

"We'll go as soon as I eat," he said. "You can relax over another cup of tea while you're waiting. This is Prescott, you know. Everything moves slower here than what you're accustomed to down in Phoenix."

Except for Brandon Hamilton, Andrea thought. He was like a steamroller, running roughshod over her sense of reasoning.

Going shopping with him was a terrible idea. The last thing she needed was to be in close proximity to the man who had caused her to behave so wantonly out of character.

She was going to get up from that table and walk out of the dining room...right now.

But, then again...

She didn't like the thought of running and hiding from Brandon Hamilton. She met challenges head-on. She came, saw, and conquered.

So, fine. She'd go shopping for a coat with Brandon, and prove to herself that she was once again in total control over her brain and body in regard to this man.

Yes, that was exactly what she would do.

Andrea settled back in her chair, picked up her cup and smiled at Brandon ever so sweetly.

"When in Rome..." she said. "I'll just sit here and enjoy my tea while you eat your Number Three."

Brandon nodded, his gaze riveted on Andrea's face.

What was she up to? he wondered. What did that strange little smile Andrea had suddenly produced mean? What was going on in that beautiful head of hers?

No, he definitely was not going to live long enough to reach a point where he understood women.

Brandon's Number Three proved to be an enormous plate-size waffle topped with a mound of whipped butter, with a little china pitcher of maple syrup on the side.

Andrea laughed when she saw the gigantic waffle.

"Is your friend Ben joining us?" she said. "I'm assuming someone is going to help you eat that incredible thing."

"Nope," Brandon said, smiling. "It's all mine, and I intend to enjoy every bite."

"Go for it." Andrea frowned slightly. "Don't you worry about calories, cholesterol, sugar rushes?"

"As much as the next person does, I suppose," Brandon said, lifting one shoulder in a shrug. He spread the butter over the waffle, then dribbled on the syrup. "I have a complete physical every year, and I'm in good shape. I'd never had a health problem until—" He stopped speaking and took a bite of the gooey offering. "Mmm. This is delicious."

"Until?" Andrea prompted.

"You know, you remind me of how I used to operate in New York City, Andrea. I worked sixteen- and eighteen-hour days and most weekends, then filled any leftover hours with a fast-track social life."

"Well, I certainly don't have a fast-track social life," she said.

Now that she thought about it, she mused, she had very few social outings at all, except for an occasional invitation to dinner or the theater. When was the last date she'd had? Two months ago? Three? Where had she gone and with whom? She honestly couldn't remember.

"Okay," Brandon said, bringing Andrea back to attention. "Forget the fast-track social life. But you *do* focus nearly entirely on your job."

"It's a career, not a job," she said a tad coolly. "A job is where you go to put in the hours so you can collect a paycheck. A career comprises hopes, dreams, goals. It requires total dedication."

"No, it doesn't," Brandon said, shaking his head. He ate more of the waffle before he spoke again. "Believe me, I used to buy into that theory myself until—" He popped another bite of waffle into his mouth.

"Brandon, you keep dropping the word *until* into the conversation, then leaving it hanging. Until…what?"

Brandon took a sip of coffee, then met Andrea's gaze directly.

"Until I had all the warnings of a heart attack waiting to do its number on me. I was very, very fortunate that I got rapped on my thick, stubborn head before the dastardly deed actually happened."

"You don't look like a candidate for a heart attack," Andrea said.

"I know, but I had to reevaluate my life-style, and my priorities. I walked away from that fast-paced existence, and here I am in Prescott, Arizona, where I grew up.''

"I see," Andrea said quietly.

"I'm very grateful to Aunt Charity for nailing me to the wall last night and telling me that I was falling into old patterns." Brandon chuckled. "Well, I sure don't have a fast-track social life here, but I *was* focusing far too much on work. I have no intention of living that way again. Not ever."

"Good for you," Andrea said, nodding.

"You're missing the whole point of this story, Andrea," he said. "You're a carbon copy of who I used to be. You've even had a loud-and-clear warning from your body that you're headed for major trouble. You're due—overdue—to take a personal inventory and make some major changes in your life-style."

"Brandon, you don't even know me," Andrea said, her voice rising. "There you sit with your holier-than-thou attitude, lecturing me on how to conduct my life, when you don't have a clue as to who I am."

"Don't I?"

"No," she said, folding her arms over her breasts. "You certainly don't."

"All right, humor me. You go into the office earlier than your staff, and stay later. You work most weekends. You break for lunch only when it includes a business meeting with a client."

"I—"

"Shh," Brandon said. "I have the floor. You have a nice apartment, or house, but it's showroom perfect, with few personal touches, because there has never been time to turn it into a warm, welcoming home.

"When you do steal a few hours for a social outing, your mind wanders and you find yourself thinking about the current project you're working on. You—"

"That's enough," Andrea said, her voice trembling slightly. "Stop it."

"Did I hit a nerve?" Brandon said, raising his eyebrows.

"That's none of your business."

Brandon leaned toward her. "Those were my arms you fainted into yesterday, Andrea. You became my business the moment that happened."

"I certainly did not. I apologized for my dramatic entrance into your hotel. It's over. Done. Forgotten. And just for the record, I did not have early warnings of a heart attack. I'm tired, that's all. And after my two-week sentence—or whatever you want to call it—here in Prescott, I'll be as good as new, full of vim and vigor again."

"So you can return to Phoenix and take up where you left off?" Brandon said. "For heaven's sake, Andrea, wake up and smell the coffee. You're headed toward physical and emotional disaster."

Andrea planted both hands flat on the table and leaned toward Brandon.

"Why on earth are you getting all in a dither about *my* life?" she said.

Brandon covered one of her hands with his and looked into her big, dark eyes.

"I don't know, Andrea," he said quietly. "I really don't know."

"Then let's consider the topic closed."

Andrea attempted to pull her hand free, but Brandon tightened his grip.

"No," he said. "It's not a closed subject. I see what you're doing to yourself, and it upsets me. I...I care about what happens to you, Andrea Cunningham. That doesn't make any more sense to me than it does to you, but it's very true.''

Andrea opened her mouth with every intention of informing Mr. Busybody Hamilton that he should quit interfering in matters that were none of his concern.

But she couldn't speak as sudden, unexpected, and very unwelcome tears closed her throat, making it impossible to say one word.

She was about to cry, Andrea thought incredulously, snapping her mouth closed. This was ridiculous. What on earth was the matter with her?

There was just…something about the way Brandon had said he *cared* about what happened to her that had caused a strange warmth to encircle her heart, threatening to push her over an emotional edge.

How long had it been since someone, anyone, had *cared* about her well-being? Years? Decades? Oh, what difference did it make? Brandon was meddling in her life and she resented his intrusion of her privacy.

But, oh, dear, Andrea thought, now he was looking at her so intently with those mesmerizing dark eyes of his, the concern, the caring, radiating so clearly, she felt as though she could reach out and touch it, wrap it around her like a warm, comforting blanket.

What was this man doing to her?

Nothing, nothing at all, she decided frantically. She was once again a victim of the fatigue and the vulnerability that exhaustion was causing.

Get a grip, Andrea Cunningham, she ordered herself. *Right now.*

''Andrea?'' Brandon said quietly.

Averting her eyes from his, she cleared her throat.

"The chamber of commerce would be proud of you, Brandon. You're a fine example of Prescott's friendly people, or whatever the town slogan is along those lines." She lifted her chin and looked at him again. "May I have my hand back please?"

A flash of anger crossed Brandon's face and shone in his eyes. He released Andrea's hand, then sank back in his chair and sighed, the sound having a definite echo of exasperation.

"Hello, darlings," Aunt Charity said, swooping down on the pair.

She was wearing a vibrant, purple satin dress with yards of material in the skirt.

"May I sit a moment?" she said, then proceeded to settle onto one of the empty chairs at the table. "How are you both this morning? Fine? Good. Are you going out? Of course, you are, or Brandon wouldn't be without his high-falutin' suit. So! You can do me a favor, if you'd be so kind. Thank you."

"Hello, Aunt Charity," Brandon said, chuckling despite his now-less-than-cheery frame of mind. "What kind of favor?"

"Well, since you've obviously taken my sterling advice and are not working today, big boy, you can pick up the music box that I ordered for Pru for Christmas. Here's the paid receipt." She smacked the piece of paper onto the table. "This will keep me from freezing my tutu off outside."

"No problem," Brandon said, picking up the paper. "We're on a mission to buy Andrea a coat. We can get the music box while we're out."

"Yep. Have fun." Charity got to her feet. "Don't hurry back. Goodbye."

"It was nice to see you, Aunt..." Andrea started, but Charity had already bustled away. "Goodness."

"I hope I have that much energy when I'm her age," Brandon said.

"I'd like to have that much energy right at this moment." Andrea looked at Brandon quickly. "Forget I said that. We're not starting over on the subject of my physical condition. I'm not stupid, Brandon. I know I'm tired, but I'm here in Prescott, doing something about it.

"Advertising is a demanding career, but I love it. A little downtime is not too much of a price to pay for the respect I've garnered in my chosen field."

"Nice speech," Brandon said, glaring at her. "Does seeing a billboard boasting your work keep you warm on cold winter nights?"

"We don't have cold winter nights in Phoenix, remember? It's very hot down in the valley."

"Lord," Brandon said, tossing his napkin onto the table. "You're a tough case, do you know that? You refuse to give an inch."

"I didn't get to where I am in my career by giving inches, Mr. Hamilton."

"Ta-ta," Prudence said, seeming to materialize out of nowhere.

"We're having a convention right here at this table," Andrea said under her breath.

Prudence's dress of the day was a moss-green wool with a high neck and long sleeves. She sat down in the chair that Charity had vacated.

"I just encountered Charity in the lobby," Prudence said, "and she informed me that you two are going shopping for a coat for Andrea. Might I prevail upon your kindness to retrieve my Christmas gift for

Charity that has arrived and is waiting to be claimed?"

"Sure," Brandon said.

"Thank you, dear," Prudence said, handing him a yellow piece of paper. "It's a music box that had to be ordered. I've already reimbursed the shop owner for it."

"We'll deliver it to your door." Brandon tucked the receipt in the pocket where he'd placed Charity's.

"Thank you so much, dear," Aunt Pru said. "Now, Andrea, dear, do be certain that you purchase a warm enough coat. You mustn't catch a chill while you're with us. Don't rush about when you're outside, either. Do conserve your energy and strength. Brandon, see to it that you share a hearty lunch with Andrea during your outing."

"Yes, ma'am," Brandon said, smiling.

"We'll be back long before lunch, Aunt Pru," Andrea said.

"Oh, my, I hope not. Brandon needs time away from this hotel. We do worry that he's working much too hard. Please don't hurry to return. You two are so good for each other. You both need to relax and enjoy yourselves. I must dash. Ta-ta."

Aunt Pru was up and gone before Andrea could echo the ta-ta.

"Well, we have our assignments," Brandon said, pushing back his chair. "Are you ready to go?"

"Yes, I guess so."

"Interesting thought, isn't it?" he said.

"What is?"

"That statement that Aunt Pru just made." Brandon got to his feet and looked down at Andrea. "She said that we are good for each other. Yes, indeed, that's a very interesting thought.''

Andrea chose not to comment as she rose to stand next to Brandon.

Interesting thought? her mind repeated.

No, she quickly corrected, it was a ridiculous thought. She and Brandon weren't *good* for each other. They did nothing but argue, and would do well not to *murder* each other while on their shopping trip.

Despite the aunties urging them not to hurry back to the hotel, Andrea was giving this outing two hours maximum.

Then she'd spend the remainder of the day in her room, reading a novel.

Alone.

Five

A little over an hour later Andrea emerged from a store wearing her new purchases, a puffy, bright red jacket, and a red and navy-blue wool hat with matching gloves.

"I look like an overripe tomato," she said, unable to curb a bubble of laughter.

"You do not," Brandon said. "You're insulting my taste. If I'd left it up to you, you would have gotten the boring beige one, or the gray, or the black. You're extremely festive in that ensemble. Besides, it was all very democratic, you know. The selection of the coat, hat and gloves was put to a vote."

"Right," Andrea said dryly. "And the woman who owns the store and had one of the votes just happens to be someone you went to high school with. The ballot box was a tad stuffed, Mr. Hamilton."

Brandon shrugged. "Whatever works. The fact remains that you can't get into the holiday spirit wearing a drab jacket, Ms. Cunningham.''

"Oh? Your coat is tan."

Brandon glanced down at his suede jacket lined with white sheepskin.

"Please, madam, bite your tongue. Don't you realize that this is a creation that literally hollers machismo? Only the mean and lean—a man's man—wear these coats. I look like a cowboy out of the Old West."

"Okay, okay," she said, raising both gloved hands. "I surrender."

"You do?" he said, grinning at her. "Terrific. Then you won't argue about the next event on our agenda."

"Picking up the music boxes for Aunt Pru and Aunt Charity? No problem."

"That's not next." Brandon grabbed one of her hands. "Come on. If we hurry, we can make the light to cross the street."

"But..."

Andrea stopped speaking as she hurried to keep up with Brandon's long-legged stride.

This was so crazy, she thought. She now owned a jacket, hat and gloves that were as out of character for her as her dumb car.

The scene in the store had been silly and...well, yes, fun. She couldn't remember when she'd laughed so much, felt so young and carefree.

Brandon and the owner of the store had ganged up on her, shouting their disapproval at her selections of somber-colored coats. She'd finally thrown up her hands in defeat and allowed the merry pair to deck her out like a radish.

If she didn't start behaving like the Andrea Cunningham she knew, there was no telling what she might do during her two-week stay in Prescott.

Andrea glanced up quickly at Brandon as he continued to urge her forward.

That was a sobering thought, she mused. She seemed to be falling more and more under the spell of this compelling, incredibly handsome, charming man.

Why wasn't she demanding that Brandon stop this nonsense, go directly to the store where the music boxes were waiting to be retrieved, then return her to the hotel?

Good question, she thought. So what was the answer? There she was, being dragged to heaven only knew where to do heaven only knew what, without a peep of protest. Why? She really didn't know.

After they'd crossed the street, Brandon left the sidewalk and tromped right into ankle-deep snow.

"What are you doing?" Andrea said. "This is snow."

"Very good," he said, chuckling. "You may go to the head of the class. You are now standing on what is known as the town square, or the plaza. That majestic building there is the county courthouse. Do note the gazebo to your right that has been decorated to look like Santa's workshop. Cute, huh?"

"Yes, yes, it is," Andrea said, sweeping her gaze over the area. "The trees look like something out of a Christmas fairy-tale book the way they're covered in snow. It's very pretty." She paused. "Did we have to *stand* in the snow to appreciate the view?"

"Yep, because we're going to build a snowman."

"What?"

"Have you ever built a snowman, Andrea?"

"No."

"Then it's my duty as a resident of Prescott to rectify that sorry situation."

Brandon stopped speaking for a moment as he looked around.

"My parents are no longer living, but when I was a kid," he said quietly, "my dad and I had a tradition. When the first big snow of the season fell, he'd bundle me up, bring me down here and we'd build a snowman on the square. My mom would have hot chocolate with marshmallows—lots of marshmallows—waiting for us when we got home."

"That's a lovely memory," Andrea said softly. "An enviable one."

Brandon nodded, then looked directly into her eyes. "Let's make a memory, Andrea. Together. We'll build a dynamite snowman."

Andrea opened her mouth to retort with an emphatic *no,* to tell Brandon that her feet were already cold, that she was an adult, not some child who was about to frolic in the snow, for mercy's sake. No, absolutely not.

Let's make a memory, Andrea. Together.

But she didn't speak as Brandon's quietly spoken words hummed in her mind, then encircled her heart with a warmth that caused her to totally forget the chilled condition of her toes.

"Yes," she whispered. "Let's make a..." A memory. A memory like none she had in the nearly empty treasure chest in her heart. A special memory. With Brandon. "A wonderful snowman."

And so they did.

And it was fun.

They were soon joined by several children, who helped roll the huge balls of snow, then lifted them into place. Everyone was slipping and sliding, falling into the wet snow, then staggering to their feet once again.

Andrea was laughing so hard that she knew she was in danger of getting the hiccups. But, oh, what fun she was having. She was helping to build an hon-est-to-goodness Frosty the Snowman for the first time, and the enchanting adventure was fabulous.

"All right," Brandon shouted, punching a fist into the air. "The head is on. It's lookin' great, team."

"I'm coming, Brandon," a woman called. "I just don't move as fast as I did in the old days."

The group turned to see a plump woman in her sixties hurrying toward them. She was wearing men's floppy galoshes, and she was clutching a heavy sweater closed over her ample breasts with one hand. She had something in her other hand.

"Martha!" Brandon said, then gave the woman a big hug when she reached them. "Andrea, this is Martha Hill. She and her husband own the café across the street there. Martha, this is Andrea Cunningham, a guest at Hamilton House. And this fine fella—" he swept one arm in the air "—is Andrea's very first snowman."

"And he's a beauty," Martha said, smiling. "I saw you out here, Brandon, and it just warmed my heart. It brought back the days when you and your daddy would be building a snowman from the first snowfall. My job in those days was to bring you a carrot for a nose, radishes for a mouth and figs for eyes. So, here I am."

"I love you," Brandon said, giving her a smacking kiss on the cheek.

Martha deposited the goodies in Brandon's cupped hands.

"Come over to the café for something hot to drink when you're finished," Martha said. "All of you. Brrr. It's cold."

Martha hurried away and Brandon poked the offerings into place on the top ball of snow.

"Oh, my," Andrea said. "He's alive now, and he looks so real and happy."

Brandon slid one arm across her shoulders and pulled her close to his side.

"Do you like him?" he said, looking down at her.

"He's wonderful," she said, meeting his gaze. "Thank you, Brandon. I won't ever forget building my first snowman."

"Good. Then we did it. We made a memory together."

"Yes. Yes, we did."

In front of the smiling snowman and the wide-eyed children, Brandon lowered his head and kissed Andrea.

He can't do this, Andrea thought. Brandon was kissing her in public, in the town square of Prescott. This was terrible. This was embarrassing. This was... divine.

This kiss was another memory they were making together.

Brandon slowly and reluctantly raised his head.

"You must be cold," he said, a gritty quality to his voice.

Not really, Andrea thought, rather dreamily. How could a person be cold when there was such all-consuming heat swirling within her? No, oh, no, she wasn't the least bit cold.

"Hey, Brandon," a man said.

Brandon turned his head in the direction of the voice, but kept Andrea tucked by his side.

"Jeff," he said. "How's it going?"

"Can't complain," the man said. "I heard you were down here building a snowman, and I came to take a picture for the paper. We'll probably save it for the special Christmas Eve issue."

Andrea blinked, bringing herself from the sensual haze she was encased in.

"A snowman is big news?" she said.

"You bet," Jeff said. "This is the first snowman of the year on the square. Okay, everyone, line up, with Frosty in the middle. Then I'll get your names."

"Oh, I don't think..." Andrea started.

"Exactly," Brandon said. "Don't think. This isn't Phoenix, Andrea. You don't have to worry about your reputation. None of your megabucks clients will see our dinky little newspaper." He frowned. "Besides, would it be all that terrible if one of the head honchos saw that you'd done something as *human* as building a snowman?"

Andrea matched Brandon's frown. "Men have far greater leeway in the corporate world, Brandon. Women have to walk the straight and narrow at all times. You must be aware of that fact from your years in that world."

"I worked with an attorney in the firm in New York who had a baby."

"Did she move up to being a partner after the birth of her child?" Andrea said.

"Well, no, but..."

Andrea poked her pink-from-the-cold nose in the air. "I rest my case."

"Hey, Brandon," Jeff said. "Am I taking a picture here or not?"

"Andrea?" Brandon said.

What should she do? she thought. There she stood, a soggy mess, having just romped in the snow like a child. She would definitely not want any of her clients to see her like this.

But Brandon was right. This was Prescott, not Phoenix. What reason would there be for any of her clients to read a small-town newspaper?

Not only that, she hadn't been behaving true to form since she'd arrived on top of this freezing cold mountain. So, what the heck.

"Yes," she said, smiling. "We're taking a picture with the most magnificent snowman ever built on the town square of Prescott, Arizona."

"Way to go," Brandon said, then dropped a quick kiss on her lips.

The picture was taken, then the group went across the street to the café. The children settled into one of the blue-leather booths, while Andrea and Brandon sat opposite each other in another.

Martha set huge mugs of hot chocolate in front of them, the surface of the steaming drinks covered in melting marshmallows.

Brandon stared at the mug.

"I know your mother always had a drink like this waiting for you and your father after you built the snowman, Brandon," Martha said quietly. "Your mother was one of my best friends, and I still miss her. When that plane your folks were on went down,

I was devastated. I hope I haven't upset you by serving you this drink."

"No, no, I'm fine." Brandon smiled at Martha. "It was a very thoughtful thing to do. Thank you, Martha."

Martha nodded and walked away.

"You're very fortunate, Brandon," Andrea said. "This whole town is like an extended family for you."

Brandon nodded. "Yes, you're right. I hadn't thought about it quite like that." He chuckled. "There's also a certain lack of privacy, too, you realize. Not much goes unnoticed and ungossiped about here. I'd say there are about twenty people who already know that I kissed a pretty lady in a red coat on the square."

"Oh," Andrea said, her eyes widening.

"Don't panic." Brandon paused. "Look, why don't you start viewing your visit here as the vacation that it is. Don't stew. Don't worry. Don't fuss. Just enjoy. Do whatever feels right at the moment. How does that idea sound?"

"I've never operated like that in my entire life." Andrea frowned, then laughed in the next instant. "Correct that. I haven't been acting true to form ever since I strolled onto the new car lot in Phoenix and bought my candy-apple-red sports car, just as bold as you please."

"You own a red sports car?" Brandon said with a hoot of laughter. "I don't believe it."

"Neither do I," she said, still smiling. "That's only one example of what exhaustion has done to my brain." Andrea paused and stared into space. "I've been behaving like a stranger even to myself. Weird. Very weird.''

"But not all bad?'' Brandon said, his smile fading as he looked at her intently.

Andrea met his gaze. "No. No, it hasn't been all bad,'' she said softly, no hint of her smile remaining.

No, not at all, she thought. Kissing Brandon, being held in his strong arms, had been wonderful.

Buying her coat, building a snowman, had been such carefree fun.

Meeting friendly people like Aunt Pru, Aunt Charity, Ben, and Jennifer, being so warmly welcomed, was so nice, so different from what she was accustomed to.

No, being in Prescott was definitely not all bad.

"So?'' Brandon said, realizing he was hardly breathing. "Will you do it? Go with the flow, live for the moment at hand, during the remainder of your stay here?''

"Well,'' Andrea began slowly. "Yes, I guess so. That's what I seem to be doing already, so if I agree to your suggestion, then maybe I won't feel so out of control, so off-kilter.'' She shook her head. "Oh, I don't know. Between my exhaustion and adjusting to the high altitude, I don't seem capable of thinking very straight. I'm not being sensible and organized, like I usually am. And apparently I don't have much choice in the matter.''

"That's fine. That's good. That's great.'' Brandon took a much-needed deep breath. "Just keep on keeping on, exactly as you are.''

"Well, at this precise moment, I'm going to the ladies' room,'' Andrea said.

"It's in the back,'' Brandon said.

Andrea slid out of the booth, and Brandon watched her until she disappeared through the designated door. He shifted his gaze to Andrea's mug of hot chocolate, then the empty place where she had been sitting.

He liked looking across the table at Andrea Cunningham, he thought. She'd only been gone a few minutes but, well, he missed her, wanted her to hurry back so he could see her smile, hear her laughter, watch the emotions that were reflected so clearly in her expressive dark eyes.

Andrea was becoming very important to him very quickly, he had to admit.

If Andrea hadn't come to Prescott, he wouldn't have built a snowman on the square, wouldn't have relived the fond memories of his father.

Now he was sharing hot chocolate and marshmallows with Andrea, bringing her into his world again, into his past, by having the traditional drink prepared by his mother after the construction of the yearly snowman with his dad.

And it felt good.

And very, very right.

It was as though there had been something missing from his existence since he'd gotten Hamilton House up and running. There had been a void, an emptiness he'd been unaware of, that he'd filled with working long hours at the hotel.

But now Andrea was here and he felt more complete, more at peace, than he could ever remember.

Brandon dragged both hands down his face.

Oh, man, he thought, what was going on here? What was Andrea doing to him? What was happening between them?

He just didn't know, but he had every intention of finding out.

Butterflies dancing.

Brandon stiffened, every muscle in his body tensing, as his mind suddenly whispered the whimsical story about the butterflies, told to him by Aunt Pru and Aunt Charity.

Was that what he wanted? he thought. To fall in love, see the butterflies dancing, have a home, be a husband and father?

His entire life would change if he chose to travel down that road. Wouldn't a man know if that journey was the one he yearned for? Maybe not, if there had been no woman to nudge awake those hidden hopes and dreams.

But what if…

Andrea.

Brandon stared at the empty place across the table, envisioning Andrea so clearly he felt as though she'd already returned to the booth.

Was *that* what was happening to him? he thought, feeling a trickle of sweat run down his chest. Was Andrea slowly but surely opening a dusty door in his heart that had been firmly closed until she'd fainted in his arms?

Brandon glanced up and saw Andrea walking toward him, her coat over her arm, a soft smile on her lips as she approached.

Was he falling in love with this woman? he thought frantically. Did he *want* to be in love with Andrea Cunningham? He had to have some answers before he went right out of his beleaguered mind.

Andrea slid into the booth, stirred the hot chocolate and took a sip.

"Mmm," she said. "Delicious and sinfully rich, with all those melted marshmallows in it." She paused. "You haven't touched your drink, Brandon."

"What?" He shook his head slightly. "Oh. Right." He lifted his mug. "To snowmen and memories."

And to butterflies dancing? he wondered. He didn't know. He just didn't know.

"Hear! Hear!" Andrea said, tapping her mug lightly against his.

They chatted about a variety of everyday topics as they finished their drinks, then they bid Martha and the children goodbye.

When they stepped outside, they discovered that it was snowing again. Andrea tipped her head back, stuck out her tongue and caught a big, lacy flake of snow.

"There," she said, laughing. "Another first. Snowflakes, however, don't taste as good as hot chocolate and marshmallows."

"Nope," Brandon said, managing to produce a small smile. "They surely don't."

Andrea cocked her head to one side and looked at him questioningly.

"Is there something wrong, Brandon?" she said. "You seem so… Oh, I don't know…tense, preoccupied, all of a sudden."

"I do?"

"Yes, you certainly do."

"Well, I…"

"Hey," a voice called. "There they are."

Brandon's head snapped around at the sound of the familiar voice.

Saved by Rizzoli, he thought.

Ben joined Andrea and Brandon where they were standing on the sidewalk in front of the café.

"Ah, the mysterious woman in the bright red coat," Ben said, grinning. "Who was well and truly kissed by Brandon Hamilton after they built a snowman on the square. And who is that woman? As I live and breathe, it's Ms. Andrea Cunningham."

"Oh, dear heaven," Andrea said, feeling a warm flush of embarrassment on her cheeks.

"You're a gossipmonger, Rizzoli," Ben said, glaring at him.

"No, I'm not," Ben said. "I'm just an attentive listener. Four people have shared this bulletin with me so far. News does travel fast in Prescott, old buddy. The snowman is a beauty, by the way. I saw it as I was walking over here for some lunch. It reminds me of the ones you used to build with your father when we were bratty little kids, Brandon."

Brandon nodded.

"It's my very first snowman," Andrea said, smiling at Ben.

"Is that a fact?" Ben said. "You've lived a far too sheltered life. We need to do something about that."

"*We* are," Brandon said. "Come on, Andrea. We have to pick up the music boxes for the aunts."

"Snow angels," Ben went on, ignoring Brandon. "You can't leave Prescott without having flopped down in the snow and created a snow angel."

Andrea laughed. "That sounds like fun—freezing, but fun. Do you like my coat, Ben? I'd definitely stand out in a crowd in this creation."

"It's stunning," Ben said. "Red is an excellent color for you to wear, and at the moment it matches the shade of your cold nose."

Andrea and Ben burst into laughter, the happy sound grating on Brandon's nerves like fingernails scratching down a chalkboard.

Where did Benjamin Rizzoli get off flirting with Andrea? Brandon fumed. Rizzoli was pouring on his Italian charm ad nauseam. Well, Ben was going to have to find his own woman, because Andrea…

Was his?

Andrea Cunningham was Brandon Hamilton's woman?

Ah, hell, he was driving himself nuts.

"That's it," Brandon said. "We're out of here."

"What's it?" Andrea said, looking up at him.

"It?" Brandon said. "Oh. Well, the weather, the snow, the temperature. You'll catch a chill if we stand here. Let's go."

"Join me for lunch?" Ben said.

"No," Brandon said quickly. "I mean, thank you, but we just had hot chocolate."

"With marshmallows," Andrea said. "It was absolutely delicious."

"I bet it was," Ben said. "How are you feeling today, Andrea?"

"She's fine," Brandon said, gripping Andrea's arm. "But she won't be if you don't put a cork in it so we can be on our way. Say goodbye, Ben."

"Goodbye," he said then hooted with laughter. "Ben."

"Corny," Brandon said, frowning.

"It was nice to see you again, Ben," Andrea said.

"The pleasure was all mine, I assure you, lovely lady," Ben said.

"*Very* corny," Brandon said. "See ya."

As Andrea and Brandon walked away, Ben folded

his arms over his chest and watched them go, a wide smile on his face.

"Fascinating," he said to no one. "Man, oh, man, I wouldn't miss this for the world. Well, better Brandon than me, and Taylor would agree with me on that score."

With a rumbly chuckle, Ben entered the café.

Six

The following days and nights seemed to fly by as Andrea fell into an extremely enjoyable routine.

She had breakfast with Brandon in the hotel dining room each morning, then they headed out to explore what he had chosen to show her that day.

They visited three museums, saw endless intriguing specialty shops where Brandon was greeted by people he knew and who welcomed Andrea with smiles and friendly warmth. Brandon took her for a drive higher into the snowy mountains, affording her a spectacular view of Prescott and the surrounding area.

Ben Rizzoli often joined them for lunch, and Andrea came to thoroughly enjoy the company of the handsome and charming Italian doctor. She laughed herself silly at the banter between Brandon and Ben, knowing that a deep, lifelong friendship was solidly in place beneath their playful squabbling.

They related tales from their mischievous youth, many of which included Jennifer Mackane.

"We still hover over Jennifer like big brothers," Andrea recalled Ben saying. "We drive her nuts at times."

"Oh," she had said, smiling. Brandon considered Jennifer his sister? That was Jennifer's role in Brandon's life? For Pete's sake, why was she registering such a sense of relief?

"Jennifer's a widow," Brandon had clarified, bringing Andrea back to attention. "She has a four-year-old son named Joey. He's a terrific kid. Ben and I, plus our buddy, Taylor Sinclair, and a couple of other guys we grew up with, are Joey's official uncles."

"He's a fortunate little boy to have all of you," Andrea'd said quietly.

She'd grown up with no one to call uncle, or aunt, or mother and father, she thought. Joey Mackane would never lack for hugs, for people to be there when he needed them. Yes, he'd lost his father, but he had an extended family who loved him. Lucky little Joey.

Stop dwelling on the past, she admonished herself. She had her career, her dream. It was hers and no one could ever take it away from her, if she stayed focused. Her career was all she needed.

Wasn't it?

Yes, of course it was. Challenge Advertising was her family, in a manner of speaking. It provided her with everything, and fulfilled her completely.

Didn't it?

On the day marking one week since she'd arrived in Prescott, Andrea remembered that it was Christmas

Eve. Instead of napping in the afternoon, as she usually did, she slipped out of the hotel and bought gifts for Brandon, the aunts, Ben, Jennifer and Joey.

Andrea also made a stop at the store where she'd purchased her coat. With the help of the owner, she selected a dress to wear to the Hamilton House employees' Christmas party that night, which Brandon had invited her to attend with him.

When she'd returned to her room, she wrapped the presents, making each as pretty and as close to perfection as she could while listening to lilting Christmas carols on the clock radio by the bed.

As she placed the gifts on the closet shelf, Andrea realized that she was actually caught up in the Christmas spirit for the first time.

And it felt wonderful.

With a smile she stretched out on the bed and stared up at the ceiling.

She began to sing a Christmas song, terribly off tune, with the radio.

Santa, she mused, was checking his list twice to see who had been naughty or nice.

Andrea sighed, frowning slightly.

She was definitely eligible for the *nice* side of the jolly old elf's list as far as her actions and behavior were concerned.

Brandon had kissed her senseless every night at her door, then walked away, to retire to his apartment at the end of the hallway.

That was how it should be, no doubt about it.

But deep within her were what might be viewed by Santa as naughty thoughts and yearnings.

She wanted to make love with Brandon Hamilton.

The heat of passion was building, growing hotter, thrumming and pulsing through her.

Andrea sighed again.

She had never felt this way before, never. Her sexual experience was limited to a few relationships in the past, with no major emotional upheavals one way or another after the fact.

But Brandon?

He was consuming her thoughts even when she wasn't with him. She could see his smile, hear his laughter so vividly, at any given second. The mere image of him in her mind's eye caused her to smile, to be filled to overflowing with emotional warmth and physical heat.

She'd learned so much about him during the hours they'd spent together. She'd adored hearing the wonderful tales of his childhood in Prescott, and Brandon's voice rang with love and respect whenever he spoke of his parents. The same dedication was evident when he interacted with Aunt Pru and Aunt Charity.

Slowly but surely she'd revealed the circumstances of the lonely years she'd spent in foster homes, trusting Brandon with her innermost secrets.

"I'm so sorry you had such an empty, lonely childhood," Brandon had said.

"Well, that was then, this is now," Andrea said. "I have my career, the people I work with, and I am very contented."

"A job doesn't take the place of a real family, Andrea."

"Yes, it does," she said firmly. "How can you argue the point, Brandon? I don't see you with a wife and bouncing a baby on your knee."

"You've got a point there," he said, nodding. "I

can't picture myself mowing the lawn, or going to PTA meetings. As much as I enjoyed my childhood, the life-style my parents had doesn't fit me.

"That's not to say I don't enjoy women's company. But a lifelong commitment to hearth, home and taking out the trash after dinner every night? No, thanks, I'll pass."

"You prefer no-strings-attached affairs that are guaranteed to end eventually," Andrea said decisively.

"That sounds a tad tacky," he said, laughing.

"But true?"

Brandon's smile faded. "Yes, I guess so. I don't dwell on the subject. I just live my life as I see fit." He paused. "Andrea, thank you for telling me about your childhood. It couldn't have been easy to recount all that. I'm honored that you shared it with me."

"You're an excellent listener," she had said, smiling at him warmly. "Even the people who I consider friends in Phoenix know nothing about my childhood."

Phoenix, Andrea mused. She honestly hadn't given the city or her demanding career much more than a moment's thought during the week she'd been in Prescott. Challenge Advertising and her lofty position there might as well have been erased from her life for the lack of attention she'd given it.

She'd been behaving exactly the way Brandon had asked her to—simply done what felt right at any given moment.

And now?

It felt very, very right to want, to need, to make love with Brandon Hamilton.

Andrea pressed her hands to her suddenly warm, flushed cheeks.

Could she do it? Take the initiative and make it clear to Brandon that she wanted to make love with him?

The Andrea Cunningham who had arrived in Prescott one week ago never would have considered doing such a thing. Nor, she supposed, would the Andrea Cunningham who would return to Phoenix soon.

But while here, she was different, acting out of character, often feeling as though she was viewing herself from afar.

Brandon knew she was leaving in another week, knew what they were sharing was temporary, which was the way he seemed to prefer his relationships with women. They were making memories together that they each could do with as they saw fit in the future.

No one was going to get hurt when Andrea packed her suitcase, checked out of Hamilton House, and drove down the mountain in her red car. This was stolen time and it had to end. Both she and Brandon knew that.

Yes, they cared for each other, but it wasn't as though they'd fallen in love.

Now that she had put the situation in perspective, all she had to do was gather enough courage to make her innermost desires known to Brandon.

"Tonight," she whispered. "Christmas Eve. A magical night, a special night, a perfect night. Yes."

A knock sounded at the door, bringing her from her thoughts. She left the bed and hurried across the room to answer the summons. A teenage boy smiled at her when she opened the door.

"Hi, Andrea," he said.

"Hello, Mickey," she said. "What brings you to my door? I'm afraid I don't need any more gas in my car."

"I know, darn it," he said. "I sure appreciate your letting me drive that slick car, though. Anyway, I'm here because Brandon asked me to hand-deliver the newspaper to you. You and your snowman on the square made the front page."

Andrea laughed. "Oh, my goodness, I forgot all about the picture the photographer took that day. Well, our marvelous snowman has since melted, so it will be fun to have a permanent record of him."

"It's starting to snow right now," Mickey said. "You can build another snowman."

"One set of frozen toes is enough. Thanks for bringing me the paper."

"You bet. Merry Christmas."

"The same to you," she said, accepting the folded newspaper.

Andrea closed the door, then started slowly toward the bed, flipping open the paper as she went. A gasp escaped from her lips and she stopped in her tracks, her eyes riveted on the front page of the newspaper.

The people at the paper had gone all out with the Christmas Eve issue, adding color and a big headline that read "Happy Holidays!" Pictures of brightly and beautifully decorated Christmas trees surrounded the large photograph in the center of the page.

Andrea moved to the bed on trembling legs. She sank onto the spread, tightly gripping the edges of the paper.

The snowman was spectacular. The children on one side of the creation were beaming with pride.

She and Brandon were standing on the other side of Frosty. Brandon was smiling at the camera and had one arm encircling Andrea's shoulders as he nestled her close to him.

Dear heaven, Andrea thought frantically, look at her. Look at the expression on her face as she gazed up at Brandon in all her soggy, snow-covered glory.

"Oh, merciful saints," she said, then pressed shaking fingertips to her lips.

There for all of Prescott and beyond to see was a full-color picture of a woman in love, who was concentrating totally on the man who had stolen her heart for all time.

There was a soft smile on her lips, and her eyes radiated a message of love as clearly as if she were shouting it from the rooftops.

"No," she said, sudden tears filling her eyes as she shook her head. "No, it isn't true. I'm not in love with Brandon. I'm not!"

Was she?

She would know if she was, wouldn't she?

Yes. Yes, of course.

But then again, *how* would she know? She had never been in love in her life.

No, this was ridiculous, insane, unacceptable. She cared for Brandon, she knew that. All right, all right, she cared *deeply* for Brandon, but—no, she had not fallen in love during her temporary stay in Prescott. Absolutely not.

Andrea set the newspaper next to her on the bed, then jumped to her feet. She began to pace the room, wringing her hands.

Calm down, Andrea, she told herself, blinking

away the unwelcome tears. She had to think, sort this through.

But if she was in love with Brandon, as that damnable picture in the paper seemingly announced to the world, she didn't want to know.

Nothing had changed. She was still leaving Prescott in a week to return to her career, her existence in Phoenix.

Yes, she cared for Brandon very much, and she would cherish the wonderful memories of him, of what they'd shared together, that she had tucked safely away in the treasure chest in her heart.

But on New Year's Day, she would pack her suitcase, settle her bill at the hotel, get into her car and drive away.

She would never see Brandon again.

A chill coursed through her as she continued to pace around the room.

No, she would never see Brandon again. Whatever feelings she might have for him would dim, fade, then finally disappear.

She had no time, no place in her life for love. Being in love and having that love returned in kind led to marriage, hearth and home, babies. She had no room for all of that. No room.

And even if she'd actually been stupid enough to have fallen in love with *him*, Brandon wasn't in love with *her*.

A man like him wouldn't be content to kiss her good-night at the door every evening, then walk blissfully away, if he was in love with her. He cared for her, yes, but he wasn't in love with her, because he'd given no indication that he wanted to *make* love with her.

Andrea stopped abruptly.

She had been determined to make love with Brandon tonight. Did she dare follow through on that brazen mission while not knowing the true depths of her feelings for him? Was that emotionally dangerous?

Andrea edged closer to the bed and peered at the photograph.

Maybe it was a trick of light, the way she just happened to look when she was half-frozen. Whatever the case, she was ignoring it.

She still wanted to make love with Brandon.

And there was still no reason why either of them would be hurt by taking that momentous step.

"Oh-hh," she said, flopping stomach-down onto the bed. "I'm driving myself crazy."

Jennifer came striding down the corridor leading from the dining room just as Ben entered the hotel. At the exact same moment, Aunt Pru and Aunt Charity emerged from the elevator.

All four were carrying the special edition of the newspaper. All four headed directly for the registration desk where Brandon was talking on the telephone.

Brandon glanced up, then did a double take as he swept his gaze over the quartet in front of the counter, all of whom were staring at him intently.

"Well, keep us posted, Jerry," Brandon said. "This is certainly worth missing the Christmas party for, isn't it? That baby will arrive when it is good and ready... Okay, we'll be waiting to hear from you. Goodbye."

Brandon replaced the receiver and smiled at the assembled group.

"That was Jerry," he said. "His wife is in the hospital in labor. The only question that remains is whether they have a Christmas Eve, or Christmas Day, baby." He paused. "You're all a bit early, aren't you? The party doesn't start for another three hours. It's at nine o'clock. Remember?"

"We remember," Jennifer said. "I don't know about the others, but I came to see you about this picture on the front page of the newspaper."

"Ditto," Ben said.

"Yes, dear," Aunt Pru said. "Charity and I came directly down when we saw this photograph after Mickey delivered the paper to us."

"You sly devil you," Aunt Charity said. "You are one fast worker, I must say."

Brandon frowned. "You've totally lost me. What are you talking about?"

"Have you looked at the picture?" Jennifer said. "Really looked at it?"

"Sure," Brandon said, shrugging. "It's great. That's one fine snowman, don't you think? My father would be proud."

"You're as dense as a rock," Ben said, shaking his head. He smacked his copy of the paper onto the counter. "Take another look."

"Perhaps, Brandon, dear," Aunt Pru said, "you might tell us what you see."

"You're all acting very weird," he said, eyeing them warily.

"Put a cork in it and do as you're told, big boy," Aunt Charity said.

Brandon shifted his confused gaze to the newspaper.

"I'll humor you," he said. "It's very sad that you all went nuts at the same time."

"Hamilton," Ben said, a warning tone to his voice.

"All right," Brandon said. "We have here a full-color spread of Christmas trees surrounding the picture of a snowman. The snowman is smiling, the kids are smiling, Andrea and I are smiling. What else? We're covered in snow, are obviously wet and cold, but don't care. That covers it."

"Dense *and* dumb as a rock," Ben said. "Hey, I'm no expert about this stuff, but even I can see it."

"See what?" Brandon said. "May I have a clue? Are we playing Twenty Questions?"

"Who wants the honors?" Jennifer said.

"Aunt Pru," Ben said, "you talk to this idiot. If I try to, I'll probably deck him."

"There's a thought," Aunt Charity said. "I'll vote for that."

"You people are starting to get on my nerves," Brandon said. "What in the hell is going on?"

"Brandon, dear," Aunt Pru said. "I must admit that I'm a bit disappointed in you."

"You are?" he said, raising his eyebrows. "What did I do?"

"It's what you didn't do, dear," Aunt Pru said. "We all saw it so clearly." She sighed. "Brandon, look at Andrea's face, her smile, her eyes, in that photograph."

Brandon glanced down at the picture, then back at Aunt Pru.

"So?" he said.

"Darling," Aunt Pru said gently. "That is a woman who is in love, gazing at the man who has captured her heart. That is the look that brings out the butterflies dancing, dear.''

"What?" Brandon snatched up the newspaper and stared at it. "I... She... What?"

"Andrea Cunningham is in love with you, you dolt," Ben said.

"Right on," Aunt Charity said. "So, hot stuff, what are you going to do about it? That's what we all want to know."

"You're crazy," Brandon said, frowning. "I'm going to have you four committed, that's what I'm going to do. Andrea isn't..." He looked at the picture again. "She is?"

"Yes, dear," Aunt Pru said. "She is."

"I wonder if Andrea realizes it?" Jennifer said, pressing one fingertip to her chin. "The dense dud here sure is operating in the dark. Do you suppose we have a matched set on our hands?"

"It wouldn't surprise me in the least," Aunt Charity said. "Do remember that Andrea has her head in a career cloud."

"Oh, heavenly days," Aunt Pru said. "Whatever shall we do?"

Brandon planted his hands flat on the counter and leaned forward.

"What you will do," he said, a muscle ticking in his tightly clenched jaw, "all of you, is disappear within the next three seconds."

The four took a step backward in perfect unison.

"Oh," Jennifer said.

"Please don't think we're meddling, dear," Aunt Pru said. "We came to speak with you about this matter out of concern and love."

"We thought you might be too stubborn and set in

your ways to see the nose in front of your face, let alone the photograph in front of your nose, which proved to be true," Aunt Charity said.

Ben coughed to smother a chuckle.

"Goodbye, people," Brandon said.

"We're outta here, ladies," Ben said. "See you at the party later, Brandon."

"Mmm," he said, glowering at the quartet.

Jennifer headed back to the dining room. Ben made a beeline for the front door. Aunt Pru and Aunt Charity bustled toward the elevator.

Brandon kept his stern expression firmly in place until he was certain the four were completely out of view. Then he took a deep, shuddering breath, pulled out the stool from beneath the counter and plunked down onto it with a thud. He stared at the picture in the newspaper.

Andrea had fallen in love with him? His mind thundered. Was it possible? Was it really true? Four people, whom he cared for, trusted and respected, had just told him that Andrea was, indeed, in love with him.

He peered closer at the photograph, then stared into space.

The week he had just spent with Andrea had been nothing short of heaven…and hell.

The heaven had come from being with her, from sharing and discovering important and meaningful details about each other.

Andrea had filled the void inside him to overflowing with an incredible warmth.

The hell was twofold.

To kiss Andrea good-night at her door each evening, then turn and walk away to enter his apartment alone had tied him in knots. He'd spent the nights tossing and turning in a bed that was suddenly too big, cold and empty.

He wanted to make love with Andrea.

The desire burned so hot that it threatened to consume him. It was like nothing he had ever experienced before.

It had taken every ounce of willpower he possessed to leave Andrea each night. He hadn't wanted to push, to run the risk of pressuring her, perhaps causing her to refuse to see him again.

Was he in love with Andrea? Did his emotions match the ones that Jennifer, Ben, and the aunts claimed that Andrea had for him?

He didn't know. But, oh, damn, the mere thought of it was terrifying. He didn't *want* to be in love. He wasn't cut out for marriage and the whole package it presented. No way.

Besides, Andrea was a guest at Hamilton House, a temporary visitor to Prescott. In one more week, she was scheduled to leave, to walk out of his life. She was a career-oriented woman, who had given no hint that she yearned for a life-style that included a husband and babies.

Brandon sighed and dragged both hands down his face.

What was the point in knowing his true feelings for Andrea? Or her for him? Even if she had fallen in love with him, she had the strength, the fortitude, to push that emotion to a dusty corner of her mind and return to her existence in Phoenix. No matter what, that was exactly what she would do.

Wouldn't she?

But what if…

Brandon stiffened, his heart racing.

What if the busybody contingent was right, and Andrea was in love with him? And what if that love was more powerful than her dedication to her career? What if he *was* in love with Andrea, told her of his feelings, and asked her to marry him, to remain by his side in Prescott as his wife? Oh, cripe, marriage? Was he nuts?

"Slow down, Hamilton," he muttered. "Just slow the hell down."

First, he had to see, sense, maybe even be told something by Andrea herself, before he could really believe she loved him.

Second, he had to know his true feelings, the depth of his caring, for Andrea.

He had to figure out whether or not he was in love with Andrea Cunningham before he went right out of his ever-lovin' mind.

And tonight was the night.

It was Christmas Eve, with its magic and miracles, a special night of wonder and awe, a night capable of producing the answers he needed so desperately.

Yes, this was the night.

Seven

At eight o'clock a retired couple, who had been close friends of Brandon's parents, arrived at the hotel as planned.

The gentleman would play Christmas carols on the piano in the lobby and the lady would take care of the reception desk while Brandon attended the Christmas party for the staff.

"We saw the delightful picture in the paper this evening, Brandon," the woman said, smiling. "I can remember when you and your father built a snowman on the square every winter."

"Mmm," Brandon said, looking at her intently. "Did you notice anything…special about that photograph?"

"You looked cold," the man said. "I'm glad it was you out there and not me."

"Yes, it was definitely nippy," Brandon said. "Anything else?"

"Well..." the woman said thoughtfully.

"Yes?" Brandon prompted, leaning toward her slightly.

"I must say that the young woman...Andrea, is it?" the woman said. "Yes, Andrea Cunningham. I must say..." Her voice trailed off.

Brandon had to bite his tongue to keep from shouting at the woman to get on with it, to say what she felt she must say.

"What about Andrea?" he said, forcing himself to smile politely.

"I do believe," she said, "that Andrea Cunningham is quite smitten with you, Brandon. There was just something about the way she was smiling and looking at you that..." She nodded. "Yes, Andrea is quite possibly in love with you."

"Oh, good Lord," Brandon said, dropping his chin to his chest.

"Pay her no mind, Brandon," the man said. "Women are silly romantics, the whole bunch of them. They can't help it, bless their matchmaking hearts. I saw that picture. Andrea looked wet and cold. Period." He paused. "Well, she did look happy about being wet and cold, which is completely nuts."

"Of course she looked happy," the woman said. "She's in love with Brandon."

"I've got to go check on the arrangements for the party," Brandon said. "Thanks for filling in tonight. Merry Christmas. Goodbye."

He hurried away before he was the recipient of any more opinions on Andrea's emotional state, wishing he'd never broached the subject of the damnable photograph in the first place.

The party was being held in a large conference room located beyond the end of the main lobby. A tall, twinkling Christmas tree stood in one corner of the room, Brandon's gifts to the employees beneath it. Tables and chairs lined the edges of the expanse, and a lush buffet was being set up along the far wall. A five-piece band was due to arrive just before nine o'clock.

Everything was under control.

Brandon headed for his apartment to shower and change for the festive event. He stepped out of the elevator on the fifth floor and walked slowly down the hallway, feeling suddenly exhausted.

He stopped in front of the door to Andrea's room and narrowed his eyes.

At that moment, he thought, he'd sell his soul for superhuman powers, particularly the ability to see through the wooden panel and be able to decipher the secrets in Andrea's mind…and heart.

"Cripe," he said, starting off again. "I'm totally losing it."

If he actually possessed those powers, he thought as he entered his apartment, he'd do well to discover what was going on in his own mind and heart first.

Andrea hummed along with the Christmas carols playing on the radio as she completed her makeup.

She'd taken a long, leisurely bubble bath, then shampooed and blow-dried her hair until it shone. She moved her head, pleased with the way her shiny hair swung then settled back into perfect place.

A touch of lipstick…

There, she thought. She was ready. All she had to do was put on her pretty new dress, slip into her heels, and she'd be prepared for Brandon to arrive to escort her to the party.

She settled on the side of the bed and smiled.

She felt wonderful…young, carefree, happy and… wonderful. She was about to attend a festive event with an extremely handsome man, and she fully intended to have a fabulous time.

"Remember, Andrea," she said, pointing one finger in the air, "don't think. Whatever you do, don't think."

Nope, during the party nary a one of the complicated, confusing thoughts would be allowed to creep forward from the back of her mind where she'd firmly pushed them.

Andrea frowned.

But what about *after* the party, when she and Brandon returned to the fifth floor, walked down the hallway and—

"No, no," she said, waving her hands in the air. "Erase that. Forget it."

She had no idea how she might behave when Brandon brought her back to her door. There was no sense in dwelling on it now. When the time came, she would simply do what felt truly right.

Brandon barked an earthy expletive, then added another for good measure as he yanked on one end of his tie.

Weeks before, he'd made the decision to wear his custom-tailored tuxedo to the employees' Christmas party. It was a way of showing his staff that they were first-class and meant enough to him that he would dress to the nines on their behalf.

But he was so edgy about spending the coming hours with Andrea that he had been transformed into Mr. Fumble Fingers. He could not, for the life of him, tie his damn tie.

"One...more...time," he said, the words measured and terse.

He flipped the silky strips this way, then that, tugged gently on the loops, then swore again when he saw the results of his efforts in the mirror.

"Great," he said dryly.

It was a smooth, even bow, as it should be. The problem was, it was lying between the edges of his collar vertically instead of horizontally.

"Forget it," he said, pulling it loose.

He could, he knew, ask one of the aunts to tie the blasted thing.

However, he was definitely in no mood to hear any more from the dear old ladies regarding the picture in the newspaper.

No, thank you, he'd pass. He wasn't going anywhere near Aunt Pru and Aunt Charity until they were a part of the crowd at the party.

So, that left asking Andrea to fix the crummy tie.

Brandon shrugged into his tuxedo jacket. Maybe the uncooperative tie was a blessing in disguise, he mused. To tend to it, Andrea would have to stand very close to him, would no doubt look up at him at some point in the procedure. That would allow him to look directly into her big, dark eyes and attempt to see the message everyone but him was capable of deciphering.

Good, he thought, smoothing the lapels of the

jacket. As of now, he was on full alert, prepared to pick up on every signal from Andrea that would give him a hint as to the true depths of her feelings for him.

He was a man with a mission.

Not only would he determine by the end of this night what Andrea's emotions were in regard to him, he would also figure out how deeply he cared for her.

Man, oh, man, no wonder he was a wired wreck.

Brandon sucked in a breath, let it out slowly, then squared his shoulders and left the apartment. Much too soon to suit his beleaguered mind he was knocking on Andrea's door.

Andrea jerked at the sound of the brisk rap on the door, then took a steadying breath.

Prince Charming had arrived, she thought rather giddily, and she, Cinderella, was about to go to the ball. Fine. She was ready. She was calm, cool and collected. She was simply going to enjoy.

She crossed the room and opened the door.

"Hello, Brandon," she said, smiling.

Oh, my goodness, she thought, look at him. He was wearing a perfectly tailored tuxedo, and he was so gorgeous he was stealing the very breath from her body. He was so tall, his shoulders so wide, his hair so thick and dark. His features appeared even more rugged above the fancy dress shirt. Magnificent.

"Come in," she said.

He couldn't "come in," Brandon thought, because he couldn't move! The directive from his brain to his feet was being short-circuited by the explosion of heated, coiling desire within him as he looked at the vision of loveliness standing before him.

Andrea's dress was a floor-length, red satin number with tiny straps—very tiny—holding it in place across her bare shoulders. It clung—oh, Lord, how it clung—to her slender figure, her breasts, her...

"Brandon?"

"What?" he said, shaking his head slightly. "Oh. Come in. Yes, I'll do that. Right now." He stepped into the room and Andrea closed the door. "Tie my tie. I mean, might I prevail upon you to fix my tie, which definitely seems to have a mind of its own?" He paused. "Andrea, you look absolutely beautiful."

"Thank you. So do you. Your friend at the store where I bought my coat helped me pick out this dress. I'm Cinderella tonight. That makes you Prince Charming. Now, let's see what I can do with your tie."

Andrea stepped close to Brandon and began her assignment.

She smelled like soap and flowers, Brandon thought hazily. His hands were tingling with the urge to caress the dewy skin of her bare shoulders. Hands that would be followed by his lips that would—

Knock it off, Hamilton, he admonished himself.

He had to pay full attention to everything that Andrea said and did, in addition to scrutinizing her eyes when the opportunity presented itself.

He thought about her earlier announcement. She was Cinderella? He was Prince Charming? Was that a significant statement? The fairy-tale couple had ended up together, pledging their love for all time. Was this a hint from Andrea about her hopes and dreams for them?

"There," Andrea said, patting the tie. She looked up at Brandon. "A bow."

Brandon narrowed his gaze and stared at Andrea intently.

"What's wrong?" she said, taking a step backward. "You're looking at me as though I have a bug on my nose."

"Oh. Sorry," he said. Nothing. Andrea's eyes were big, dark and beautiful, but beyond that...nothing. There was no neon sign flashing in them, telling him what he needed to know. "Shall we go?"

"All right," she said. "I just need to get my purse. I'm looking forward to this evening so very much."

Why? Brandon thought. What part of the event was Andrea anticipating with such excitement ringing in her voice? The buffet dinner? The music? The dancing? Seeing Ben?

Ben Rizzoli had better show up at the party with a date in tow, he thought, because Andrea Cunningham was with Brandon Hamilton tonight, by damn.

Cripe, Brandon thought. At this rate he was going to be a babbling idiot within the hour. He'd really prefer to turn off his mind and just enjoy Andrea's company. But he couldn't do that. Too much was at stake. The evening ahead was far too important.

Stay alert, Hamilton, he told himself as he and Andrea left the room.

In the hallway, Brandon shot a quick glance in the direction of the aunts' apartment door, hoping to the heavens that they wouldn't suddenly appear and pounce on him. He hustled Andrea into the elevator and pressed the proper button with more force than was necessary.

"Are you tense about this party, Brandon?" Andrea said as the elevator doors swished closed. "You seem rather uptight."

"I do? Well, I... Well, yes, the party. I want everything to go smoothly. The staff of Hamilton House deserves the best that I can offer."

"I'm sure it will be perfect," she said pleasantly. "You give everything you do your total effort and dedication." Every kiss, every touch, every smile. Oh, my, imagine what it would be like to make love with this man. "I can vouch for that."

"You can?" he said, looking down at her.

"Certainly," she said, smiling. "I was there when you gave your all to building the snowman on the square, remember? Our Frosty definitely received total dedication and concentration."

Brandon laughed and Andrea joined him, the merry sound filling the elevator to overflowing and following them into the lobby, where the lovely piano music was being played with expertise.

With almost everyone on the staff having brought someone special to the party, the conference room soon held close to a hundred and fifty people dressed in their finery. The atmosphere was crackling with excitement and good cheer, the noise level high.

Plates were heaped with delicious food, and Brandon and Andrea found places to sit at a table with Aunt Pru, Aunt Charity, Jennifer and Ben. Neither Ben nor Jennifer had an escort with them.

"Why don't you have a date?" Brandon said to Ben, speaking close to Ben's ear so no one else could hear the question.

Ben shrugged. "I just never got around to asking anyone to attend this shindig with me."

"Who do you plan to dance with?" Brandon said, frowning.

"I don't know," Ben said. "The aunties, Jennifer...Andrea."

"Mmm," Brandon said, glaring at him.

Ben laughed and shook his head. "You're a goner, Hamilton. Why don't you just admit it? You're a very lucky man, you know."

"I'm not having this discussion," Brandon said. "Eat your dinner."

Ben chuckled, then directed his attention to Andrea. "Ms. Cunningham," he said. "You look lovely this evening, if I may be so bold as to say so."

"Thank you, Dr. Rizzoli," she said, smiling and dipping her head slightly.

"As do you, Jennifer," Ben went on. "And you, Aunt Pru, Aunt Charity."

"Thank you, dear," Aunt Pru said.

"What about me?" Brandon said. "Aren't you going to lay some of that syrupy sweet junk on me, Ben?"

"You look like a penguin," Ben said.

"But a dashing penguin," Aunt Pru said.

Everyone laughed, including Brandon, and the mood was set. They consumed their meals with friendly banter.

A short time later, the dishes were whisked away by members of the staff who had volunteered to accomplish the chore while attending the party. The buffet table was removed to allow more space for dancing.

Brandon went to the front of the room and made a short speech, wishing everyone a happy holiday and expressing his gratitude for all of the hard work that had been put in to making Hamilton House a successful endeavor.

Mickey came forward wearing a bright red Santa Claus hat and assisted Brandon in passing out the gifts from beneath the tree.

Just as Brandon signaled for the lights to be dimmed so the dancing could commence, the woman who was tending to the registration desk rushed in and handed Brandon a slip of paper.

"All right," Brandon said, after reading the message. "Jerry and his wife have a Christmas Eve baby boy. Seven pounds, six ounces. His name is Nickalaus Gerald."

A round of applause went up in honor of the new arrival.

"Let the dancing begin," Brandon said. "Again, Merry Christmas to all of you, and every best in the new year to come."

The crowd cheered as he made his way back to the table.

A Christmas Eve baby, Andrea thought, her gaze riveted on Brandon as he approached. A miracle. A tiny, beautiful baby boy.

What would it be like to hold an infant in her arms, a child created with the man she loved?

If she'd ever yearned for a child in the past, it must have been a fleeting thought as she certainly didn't remember it.

A baby. Why was she dwelling on the subject now? Was her biological clock picking this moment to start ticking? Or was it because of Brandon Hamilton and her ever-growing feelings for him that she absolutely, positively, refused to address?

Oh, Andrea, please, she thought, *stop thinking.*

Brandon reached the table and extended a hand to Andrea as the band began to play a waltz.

"May I have this dance, Andrea?" he said, no hint of a smile on his face.

"Yes," she whispered, then placed her hand in his.

As Andrea and Brandon made their way to the center of the room, Jennifer sighed.

"Oh, this is so romantic," she said. "Andrea and Brandon are such a marvelous couple, aren't they? He's so handsome and she's so pretty. They look sensational together."

"Looks won't mean diddly," Aunt Charity said, "if they don't come out of the ether."

"You've got that straight, Aunt Charity," Ben said, nodding.

"Wouldn't you like to have a crystal ball," Aunt Pru said, "to see what the future will bring?"

"No," Ben said sharply.

"Ben?" Jennifer said, frowning.

He sighed. "I'm sorry, Aunt Pru. I didn't mean to be rude. Come on, Jennifer. Let's dance."

As Jennifer and Ben left the table, Prudence and Charity exchanged frowning expressions.

"Something is troubling our Ben, Charity," Pru said.

"Yes, you're right," Charity said. "And Jennifer has no business being at a party alone. And Andrea and Brandon are liable to mess up what they might have together. Our young people are all very complicated."

"Indeed they are," Prudence said. "Oh, Charity, I do so fear that the butterflies will dance, and no one will see them."

Eight

Andrea felt as though it was taking an eternity to weave through the tables to reach the dance floor with Brandon.

She was acutely aware of his masculine presence behind her as they made their way forward. He was so tall and strong, enveloping her in a nearly tangible haze of sensuality.

Heat was growing steadily within her, swirling, thrumming, beginning to settle low in her body with a pulsing cadence, as she anticipated the moment when she would step into Brandon's embrace.

Hurry, her mind and body demanded. They were moving in tormentingly slow motion. Her skin was tingling. Her heart was beating with a wild tempo. *Hurry.*

The dreamy music of the waltz beckoned.

Brandon curled his hands into tight fists at his sides

to keep from reaching out to touch Andrea as she walked in front of him.

Lord, he thought, the distance from their table to the dance floor had turned into the length of an enormous football field. Heat was coiling low in his body, hot, so damn hot, and he could feel a trickle of sweat slithering down his back.

Go faster, Andrea, he mentally directed. *Faster.*

Then at last, *at last,* they were there.

Andrea stepped onto the crowded wooden floor, then stopped and turned to meet Brandon's gaze as he joined her. They stood statue-still, inches apart, not touching.

The room, the people, the chattering noise, faded into oblivion as a sensuous mist encircled them. There was only the two of them, and the beautiful music.

Brandon lifted his arms slowly and Andrea floated into his welcoming embrace, a soft sigh of pleasure escaping from her lips.

Brandon closed his eyes for a moment to savor the long awaited sensation of Andrea's slender body nestling against him.

Heat rocketed through him and he welcomed it, feeling vitally alive, powerful and male. Andrea was so delicate, so feminine, her womanly contours complementing his ruggedness to perfection.

They began to sway in time to the waltz.

The song ended, another began, and Andrea and Brandon danced on and on.

"I can't even remember when I last danced," Andrea said finally. "I apologize in advance in case I step on your toes."

"I doubt that you will," Brandon said. "I think

dancing is one of those things you don't forget how to do, just like…''

"Riding a bicycle," they said in unison.

Andrea tipped her head back to smile up at Brandon.

"Thank you," she said softly.

"For what?"

"Tonight, this very special night. I'm having a wonderful time." Andrea's smile faded. "We're making more memories for me to tuck away in the treasure chest in my heart."

Brandon nodded. "Yes, we are. I like the way you put it…the treasure chest in your heart. That's nice, very nice."

"Mmm," she said, then cradled her head on Brandon's shoulder again. "It's hard to believe I've only been in Prescott a week. So much has happened since I wobbled through the doors of Hamilton House and fainted dead away."

"That's true," Brandon said. "A great deal has taken place."

But what was Andrea referring to? he wondered. During the week had she fallen in love? With him?

Was Andrea scrutinizing her life, contemplating what it might be like to stay in Prescott by his side, as his wife?

No, she wouldn't allow herself to have such fantasies, based on unknowns. She had no idea how he felt about her. She wouldn't envision a forever with him without being assured of his love for her.

A forever with Andrea?

A house that would be transformed into a home? A baby created from the exquisite lovemaking they would share in the darkness of night?

Was that what he wanted?

Was he in love with Andrea Cunningham?

An eerie fog seemed to descend around Brandon, causing a chill to course through him. He blinked, trying desperately to see Andrea where she was held safely in his arms, but he was unable to find her in the denseness of the cloud surrounding him. She was slipping from his grasp, disappearing into the fog.

Andrea was gone.

And he was alone, totally alone.

Vivid images paraded ruthlessly before his mental vision. He saw himself at the hotel registration desk, then in his empty apartment, searching desperately for something he couldn't find, knowing he needed the elusive entity to be complete, whole, fulfilled.

The scene repeated itself in stark, dark pictures. The desk, the apartment, the futile search. The emptiness. The loneliness. The pain.

No!

"Brandon?"

Andrea's whisper-soft voice calling his name caused the fog to dissipate. He was back at the Christmas party, could hear the music, the din of voices, could see and feel Andrea in his arms, thank God.

Dots of sweat beaded his brow.

He looked down at the woman in his embrace, who was gazing up at him with an expression that was a combination of confusion and concern.

And he knew.

At that moment, on the magical night of Christmas Eve, Brandon Hamilton knew he was falling deeply and irrevocably in love with Andrea Cunningham.

"Brandon?" Andrea repeated. "Is something wrong? Are you all right?"

"Am I all right?" he echoed. Hell, no, he wasn't all right. He didn't want any part of the emotional trip he was on. Somehow, he had to stop this ride and get off. But in the meantime, this was a party, so he'd fake it. "Yes, Andrea, I'm fine. I'm on top of the world."

He spun her around and she laughed in delight.

"Are we trading in our titles of Cinderella and Prince Charming?" she said, smiling. "Are we to be Ginger and Fred now?"

"No, ma'am," Brandon said, managing to produce a small smile. "We are definitely still Prince Charming and Cinderella."

Andrea stumbled slightly and Brandon chuckled as he caught her, bringing her even closer to him.

"Be careful there, Cinderella," he said. "If *I* step on *your* toes, I might shatter your glass slippers."

"Heaven forbid," she said, forcing a lightness to her voice that she definitely didn't feel.

Shattered. That was how she'd suddenly felt when Brandon said they were to remain in the roles of Cinderella and Prince Charming.

Cinderella, whose night of magic and wonder had ended abruptly at midnight, flinging her back into the stark, lonely world of her reality. She had gone to the ball and danced in the arms of the handsome prince on stolen time.

Message received, Brandon, Andrea thought. He was making it crystal clear that what they were sharing was temporary. It would all end when she left in one more week.

Andrea took a deep breath and let it out slowly.

She was all right now, back in emotional control. Brandon wasn't telling her anything that she didn't already know. But she still intended to do whatever felt right at the moment when Brandon returned her to her door.

Lord, Brandon thought. He'd nearly died on the spot when Andrea had taken the deep breath that had caused her breasts to crush more firmly against his chest.

He'd had to stifle a groan of need that had threatened to erupt. He was going up in heated flames of desire for this woman in his arms.

The woman he was falling in love with, despite his fierce determination not to.

What an incredible thing, he thought. What a momentous event. He was honest-to-goodness falling in love for the first time in his life.

If this was a perfect world, he'd be on cloud nine. He'd be the kind of man who had been searching for, and had now found, the woman of his dreams, his future wife and mother of his children.

If this was a perfect world, they would have it all, together. A real home. Children. Hamilton House. Andrea's own advertising firm in Prescott.

And love.

Love that would withstand the rigors of time, the ups and downs, the sunshine days as well as those that might be a tad cloudy. Forever love, until death parted them.

What was that nonsensical thing the aunts had gone on about? Butterflies. Yes, that was it. Because they were in love with each other, he and Andrea would see the butterflies dancing.

Yes, that was how it would be if this was a world of perfection.

But it wasn't.

Andrea was dedicated to her career to the exclusion of everything, and everyone, else. Even if she *was* in love with him, as those who'd seen the picture in the newspaper believed, she'd probably walk away from that love, ignore it, return to Phoenix and never look back.

And him? He wasn't the I-love-you-so-marry-me-kind. He didn't have enough hours in the day to devote to a wife and family. There wasn't time to build snowmen on the square with his son, sit on the porch in blissful contentment with his wife and watch the stars blink in a summer sky, have the kind of marriage that his parents had enjoyed.

He'd known the truth for many years, and tailored his social life accordingly. He moved in the fast lane, never stopping to smell the flowers, because that was how his life was structured—

Brandon stumbled, then steadied, keeping Andrea nestled close to him as they continued to sway to the music.

Dear Lord, he thought as beads of sweat dotted his brow. *Everything* suddenly became very clear to him. He'd been hiding.

Aunt Charity had jumped on his case because he was still operating *physically* the way he had in New York. What was hitting him now, like a ton of bricks, was that he was doing the same thing on an emotional level, viewing Andrea, his feelings for her, what they could have together, through the eyes of a man who had buried his hopes and dreams because of the pressures of the big city.

But he wasn't in New York anymore.

He was home.

He was free to live, and free to dream, and free to love the woman of his heart.

Andrea.

"Andrea," he said, not realizing he'd spoken aloud.

She lifted her head slowly from where she cradled it on his chest and gazed up at him.

"Yes?" she said softly.

Free, Brandon's mind echoed as he looked directly into Andrea's dark eyes. Free to love. And he did. Oh, Lord, yes, he loved this woman. That wasn't terrifying. It was wonderful, almost beyond belief.

He wanted it all. A wife. A home. Children, whose joyous laughter would fill that home to overflowing. He wanted to see, with Andrea, the butterflies dancing.

"Brandon?" Andrea said, looking at him questioningly.

"What? Oh. Are you still having a nice time?"

"My goodness, yes," she said, smiling. "I can't remember when I've enjoyed myself so much." She paused. "You know, when I first arrived in Prescott and began to realize that everyone knows everyone else's business, I thought it was rather...oh, stifling, a continuous invasion of privacy."

"And now?" Brandon said, hardly breathing.

"I don't feel that way anymore. The people here are like a big, warm and welcoming family. It disturbed me initially only because I've never experienced anything remotely close to a loving family. You're very fortunate to live here, Brandon. Prescott is a very special, very rare, little town. I adore it."

Then stay! Brandon's mind hollered. *Marry me,*

and remain by my side until death parts us. Ah, Andrea, I love you so much.

Whoa, Hamilton, he ordered himself. Slow down. He'd gotten part of the answers to his multitude of questions, but there was a muddled mess remaining in his brain.

Did Andrea truly love him? Would she consider giving up her career in Phoenix? Could she even envision a permanent future with him?

Maybe not, because she didn't have a clue as to how he truly felt about her. He wanted to tell her now, right now, that he would love her until he took his last breath.

He wanted to shout for everyone in that room to pay attention as he told them that he was in love with Andrea.

But, no, he mustn't do that. He was treading on fragile ground, had to move carefully, so as not to frighten Andrea away.

When they were alone later that night, he'd look directly into Andrea's big, beautiful eyes and tell her that he loved her. Then he would ask her to marry him, to be his life's partner.

Everyone, except dense him, was convinced that Andrea loved him after seeing the picture in the paper. He was counting on their being right, hanging on to that belief like a lifeline.

In the meantime, he'd given Andrea a hint as to the depths of his feelings for her. He'd made it clear that they were, indeed, Cinderella and Prince Charming, who had found happiness together for all time.

Had Andrea picked up on the reference to Cinderella and the Prince? Brandon wondered. Well, sure she had. She was a sharp, intelligent woman. She knew that Cindy and the Prince had overcome the obstacles in their path and made a commitment to forever. Andrea probably wouldn't be all that surprised when he declared his love and proposed to her later that night.

"Well, good," Brandon said. "I'm very pleased that you like Prescott, because I think it's close to perfect. In fact, life itself is as close to perfection as it can possibly get."

"It is?"

"Yep," he said, nodding. "Know why?"

"No."

"Because, my sweet Andrea," Brandon said, smiling. "Santa Claus is coming tonight."

Andrea laughed, Brandon tightened his hold on her, and they danced on and on.

During the next hour Ben stepped up and demanded a chance to dance with Andrea. She also danced with the head chef and with Mickey, while Brandon was partnered with the aunts, then Jennifer.

At eleven o'clock, Prudence and Charity bid everyone good-night. Aunt Pru repeated an earlier invitation to Andrea to join her and Aunt Charity for Christmas breakfast in their apartment the next morning.

Ten minutes later Jennifer headed for home, followed by Ben ten minutes after that. Others were leaving the party, as well, calling out a cheerful "Merry Christmas," instead of goodbyes.

Andrea and Brandon remained at the table, Brandon smiling and waving as the people left the room.

"Well," he said, nodding, "I'm pleased with how things went. I think everyone had a good time."

"I'm sure they did," Andrea said. "It was a marvelous party. Do you have to stay to close up the room?''

''No. Harry, the head of maintenance, volunteered for that job.''

Andrea glanced at the clock on the wall.

Fifteen minutes until midnight, she thought. She was still Cinderella. That was who she wished to be when she reached the fifth floor with Brandon. He wanted her in that role, too. No-strings-attached Cinderella.

''I'd like to leave now, Brandon, if you don't mind,'' she said. ''Glass slippers are hard on toes.''

''Are you saying that your feet hurt?'' Brandon laughed. ''That's what you get for dancing every dance.''

''It's a small price to pay,'' she said, rising. ''I enjoyed every minute.''

Brandon got to his feet, signaled to Harry and received a salute in return.

''The band will play a couple more songs,'' Brandon said as he and Andrea left the room, ''and then that will be that. I'm chalking this event up as having been a success.'' He paused. ''Hey, it's almost Christmas.''

But it was still Christmas Eve, Andrea thought, and she was still Cinderella.

As they rode up in the elevator, a sense of peacefulness touched her mind, her heart and soul.

This was her night, stolen out of time, and she knew, with no trepidation or doubt, that she wanted to make love with Brandon Hamilton. Yes, it was right, so very, very right.

No one would be hurt by taking this momentous step, she mused. Brandon had made his feelings very clear. She was here now, and the memories they made together would be theirs to keep if they chose to do so.

When she left Prescott, she'd never see Brandon again, but this night, this Christmas Eve night, was theirs.

They stepped out of the elevator on the fifth floor and walked down the hallway.

I love you, Andrea, Brandon's mind hammered. *I want you to be my wife, my partner in life, the mother of my children. Stay by my side, sweet Andrea, forever. We'll have a happy ending to our story, just like Cinderella and the Prince.*

Tell her, Hamilton. Tell Andrea that you're in love with her, and that you wish to make love with her. Damn it, tell her.

Brandon slowed as they approached Andrea's door, swallowing heavily as he prepared himself to deliver the most important speech he'd ever make in his life.

He blinked in confusion as Andrea passed her room and continued down the corridor. He hurried to catch up with her. She finally halted in front of the door to his apartment, then turned to face him.

She was suddenly so nervous her knees were trembling. She'd never done *anything* like this before, never been so aggressive and…wanton? Naughty?

No, she refused to admonish herself for what she was about to do. This decision was right. She would have no regrets—none—in the light of Christmas Day.

"Brandon," she said, looking directly into his dark eyes. "It's not yet midnight. I'm still Cinderella and you're Prince Charming, and I understand completely what that means."

"You do?" he said, his heart beginning to beat wildly. Andrea had understood what he'd meant when he'd told her they were to remain being Cindy and the Prince. Andrea Cunningham was actually in love with him, just as he was in love with her. "Ah, Andrea, I..."

"Shh," she said, placing one fingertip softly against his lips. "There's no misunderstanding between us, so no one can get hurt." She took a wobbly breath. "Brandon, I want to make love with you, I truly do."

Desire exploded within Brandon with such force, such heat, that he had to close his eyes for a moment to regain control of his body.

"And I want you," he said, his voice raspy.

He managed to retrieve his key from his pocket, inserted it in the lock on the second attempt, then pushed the door open. A small lamp cast a golden glow over the living room.

Andrea entered, her gaze sweeping over the attractive room that had been decorated in a combination of antiques and more modern, large pieces of furniture befitting a man of Brandon's size.

Brandon closed the door, shoved the key into his pocket, flipped the lock shut, then stepped in front of Andrea. She took a step backward, thudding against the door. Brandon braced his hands on the door on either side of her head and looked into her eyes, his own eyes smoldering with passion.

"You're sure?" he said. *You really love me?*

"I'm positive," she whispered. *I want to make love with you.*

Brandon leaned closer, his body only mere inches away from Andrea's, and he brushed his lips over hers. A shiver coursed through Andrea as she kept her arms straight at her sides.

Brandon outlined her lips with the tip of his tongue. Andrea curled her fingers into the satin material of her dress.

He trailed a ribbon of tantalizing kisses along her slender throat. She heard the echo of her own racing heartbeat in her ears.

"Brandon," she whispered.

"Tell me," he said hoarsely. *Tell me you love me.*

"I want you."

"I..." Brandon started, then stopped.

No, he thought, he'd wait to say the words, to declare his love, just as Andrea was. Those commitments to forever mustn't get caught up in the heat of the moment, in the raging desire consuming them.

He kissed her, deeply, his tongue parting her lips and delving into the sweet darkness of her mouth to find her tongue, stroking it in a sensuous rhythm.

Andrea's arms floated upward to encircle Brandon's neck as she moved away from the door to nestle against his aroused body. He held her close, then closer yet, his hands skimming over the feminine slope of her hips to urge her nearer.

Brandon lifted his head to take a sharp breath, then slanted his mouth in the opposite direction, capturing Andrea's lips once more. She clung to his shoulders as her trembling legs threatened to refuse to support her.

They were on fire. The flames of desire licked throughout them, heightening passions to a fever pitch like nothing they'd experienced before.

Brandon broke the kiss, his breathing rough.

"Andrea."

"Yes," she whispered, then shivered with need. "Oh, yes."

Brandon swung her up into his arms and carried her across the living room to the bedroom beyond. He set her on her feet next to the king-size bed, the lamp in the living room creating a soft, rosy hue in the room.

Brandon cradled Andrea's face in his hands and kissed her gently, so reverently, that unexpected tears prickled at the backs of her eyes.

He looked at her for a long, heart-stopping moment, then slipped the straps of her dress off of her shoulders. Andrea allowed the satin material to fall free, pooling at her feet to reveal a pale pink, strapless lace teddy that clung seductively to her dewy skin.

"Exquisite," Brandon said, his voice sounding strange to his own ears.

He began to shed his cumbersome tuxedo with visibly trembling hands. Andrea skimmed the teddy down, then stepped free of the jumble of clothes. Brandon flung his garments away, not caring where they landed.

Then they stopped, standing still a foot apart, naked before each other. Eyes roamed, savoring all that they saw.

"You're the most magnificent man I've ever seen," Andrea said, meeting Brandon's heated gaze again.

"And you're the most beautiful woman," he said.

He went to the bed, swept back the blankets, then turned to Andrea, lifting her into his arms. He settled her in the center of the blue sheets and followed her down, stretching out next to her before catching his weight on one forearm.

The journey of discovery began. They kissed, touched, caressed, with awe, with wonder. They were alone in a magical world they were creating with each beat of their racing hearts. It was ecstasy.

Brandon drew the sweet flesh of one of Andrea's breasts into his mouth, laving the nipple into a taut bud. She sank her fingers into his thick hair, pressing his head more firmly to her, rejoicing in the sensations swirling within her.

He moved to the other breast, as he splayed one hand on her flat stomach, then lower and lower yet, finding the moist heat of her femininity.

"Oh, Brandon," Andrea said, nearly sobbing. "Please. I want you so much."

He moved over her, supporting his weight on quivering arms, then entered her, bringing her all that he was, filling her.

"Oh, my," she said with a sigh of womanly pleasure. "Oh, Brandon."

Brandon began the dance, slowly at first, then increasing the tempo. Andrea raised her hips and matched his rhythm in total synchronization.

The heat coiled tighter, building, taking them up and away, higher and higher, then flinging them into exquisite oblivion.

"Brandon!"

"Yes! Ah, Andrea."

They hovered in the place where they had gone, not wishing to return. Slowly, slowly, they drifted back, sated, complete.

Brandon shifted off of Andrea and lay close to her side, weaving his fingers through her tousled, silky hair.

"Perfect," he said quietly.

"Yes," she said. "Perfect."

I love you, Andrea, Brandon whispered in his mind. He wanted to tell her, seal what they had just shared with his declaration of love.

But, no. He'd wait. To say the words now was too clichéd, like a script from a romantic movie. A man makes love to a woman, then blurts out his statement of "I love you." No. What he had with Andrea was too rare, special, to be allowed to even hint of the ordinary. He'd wait.

"Mmm," Andrea said. "I'm so sleepy."

"Then sleep, Cinderella." Brandon kissed her on the forehead.

Cinderella, Andrea thought hazily. Yes, that was who she was. She had to remember, must not forget that.

Brandon glanced at the clock.

"Andrea?"

"Hmm?"

"Merry Christmas."

Nine

The telephone on the nightstand next to the bed rang early the next morning, jarring Brandon awake. He reached out and snatched up the receiver.

"Yes?" he said quietly, glancing quickly at Andrea where she slept peacefully next to him.

"This is Ryan at the desk. Sorry to bother you so early, Brandon, but I have a problem here. A couple who were due to arrive this afternoon are standing in front of me right now. They drove all night so they could surprise their family on Christmas morning, but we don't have an empty room to put them in."

"All right," Brandon said. "I'll be down in a few minutes to see what I can do."

"Thanks," Ryan said. "Oh. Merry Christmas."

"Mmm," Brandon said, frowning as he replaced the receiver.

Damn, he thought, this was definitely not how he'd

intended to start the day. His plan had been to bring Andrea a hot cup of coffee, kiss her awake, then wait until the caffeine had accomplished its assignment.

When he was assured that Andrea was her usual, smiling self, he would have looked directly into her eyes, declared his love for her and asked her to marry him.

The only thing missing from the proposal was an engagement ring, but he'd rectify that at the earliest opportunity. They'd go to the aunts for Christmas breakfast and announce their intention to be married as soon as possible.

So much for that grand scheme, Brandon thought, leaving the bed. He'd have to think of a fresh idea. One thing was certain, though. On this Christmas morning, he would propose to Andrea Cunningham.

Brandon started toward the bathroom, then stopped, retracing his steps to stand next to the bed and gaze at Andrea.

Incredible. That was what their night together had been…incredible. For the first time in his life he'd been intimate with a woman he loved and who loved him in return. His very own Cinderella.

The lovemaking he'd shared with Andrea was so special, rare, wonderful, like nothing he'd experienced before.

They'd both awakened in the night, as though nudged by an invisible hand, then reached for the other eagerly. Their joining had been sweet and slow, intoxicating, and sensational.

Lord, how he loved this woman.

How very right she looked sleeping there in his bed, where she belonged.

And where *he* belonged, Brandon thought, spinning on his heel and striding toward the bathroom.

He showered and shaved as quickly and as quietly as possible, then dressed in black slacks and a royal-blue sweater. He indulged in one more long look at Andrea, then left the room.

With any luck he'd solve the problem of the early arriving guests in a jiffy, and just might be able to return to the apartment before Andrea even knew he'd been gone.

He could reinstate his original plan of kiss, coffee and "I love you. Will you marry me?"

But luck was not on Brandon's side.

The couple waiting at the registration desk proved to be extremely difficult to deal with.

No, they didn't want to leave their luggage in a safe place at Hamilton House and proceed to their destination to surprise their family. They wanted to shower and change into fresh, festive clothes.

Yes, they realized they had arrived early, but the hotels they were accustomed to always accommodated them if they changed their schedule a bit. Was this, or was this not, a first-class establishment? One that they might, or might not, recommend to their many friends?

Brandon gritted his teeth and searched his mind for a solution to the dilemma, wondering if one of the alternatives might be to strangle these unreasonable, demanding people?

Andrea stirred, yawned, opened her eyes, then turned her head, frowning as she saw that Brandon wasn't next to her in the bed. She sat up, clutching the sheet over her bare breasts.

"Brandon?" she called.

He wasn't in the apartment, she realized. Where on earth could he have gone? Well, he was the owner of Hamilton House. There was no telling what kind of emergency he might have been summoned to tend to.

Satisfied with her deduction, Andrea flopped back onto the pillow and stretched leisurely.

Her body was tender in places she'd nearly forgotten were there, she thought, smiling. Oh, how glorious their lovemaking had been. What a magnificent and considerate lover Brandon was, assuring her pleasure before seeking his own release.

What had Brandon said? Oh, yes, he had declared their joining as being "perfect," and that was true, wondrously true.

Andrea sighed in contentment, but her euphoric mood began to fade as a niggling little voice started to whisper in her mind.

Christmas Eve was over. The clock had struck midnight, and the ball, as well as the Cinderella who had attended it, were no more. It was time for a reality check.

She had no regrets about the night before. Quite the opposite. She would cherish the memories of making love with Brandon, keep them safely in the treasure chest in her heart forever.

Andrea turned her head to look at the pillow next to her that still held the indentation from Brandon's head.

She missed him, she thought. She wanted him suddenly to materialize so she could reach out and touch him, kiss him, feel his powerful arms pulling her close to his magnificent naked body.

She wanted to make love with Brandon now, right

this minute, soar with him to that place of pure ecstasy where she could travel to only with him.

Yes, she missed him.

Andrea shifted her gaze to the ceiling and frowned.

This was *not* good, she thought. If she missed
Brandon now, when he was in the hotel someplace
taking care of an important matter, what would it be
like when she left Prescott next week and returned to
Phoenix?

Would tears flow in the darkness of night as she
tossed and turned in her lonely bed, aching for him?

Would he consume her thoughts as she went
through each day?

Would she look for him in crowds, even though
she knew he wasn't there?

Would she snatch up the telephone every time it
rang, with the hope of hearing his voice?

No, no, that was silly, all of it. Those were things
a woman in love did, and she was *not* in love with
Brandon Hamilton.

Was she?

Andrea sat up, wrapped her arms around her knees
and rested her chin on top.

She was playing emotional ostrich, she admitted to
herself. She was refusing to discover the truth—whatever it was—of how deeply her feelings for Brandon
went.

A chill suddenly swept through Andrea, and she
felt as though a dark cloud had settled over her,
threatening to obliterate the sunshine mood she'd
awakened with.

She was registering a strange sense of déjà vu. It
was as though she had somehow been on this emo-

tional road before and had then, as now, refused to listen to her inner voice.

"That's ridiculous," she said aloud, raising her head from her knees. "Impossible."

She cared more for Brandon than she had for any man she'd ever been involved with. There was no déjà vu in that. Her relationship with Brandon wasn't remotely close to anything she'd felt, or done, before.

Then why, why, why, couldn't she shake this dark, chilling thought?

"This is crazy," she said with an unladylike snort of disgust. "Just forget it, Andrea. You should never think before you've had your first cup of coffee."

She glanced over at the clock on the nightstand.

It was getting late, she thought. She and Brandon were due at Aunt Pru and Aunt Charity's apartment for Christmas morning breakfast.

As much as she'd prefer to wait for Brandon in his bed, there just wasn't time. She had to go to her own room to shower and put on fresh clothes.

Suddenly Andrea laughed.

She was about to skulk down the hallway, wearing last night's dress, hoping that no one saw her before she was safely behind her own door. She'd never done anything like *that* before. She would be able to add "skulking" to that long list of "firsts" she was experiencing in Prescott.

"Oh, well." She shrugged, slipped off the bed, then reached for the wrinkled dress where it lay on the floor. "Go for it."

Brandon trudged slowly up the flights of stairs that would take him to the fifth floor.

A glowering glance at his watch told him that Andrea was no doubt long gone from his apartment, and was probably already sipping tea with the aunts.

So much for his plan to propose to Andrea while they were still alone, then announcing their coming marriage when they arrived at Aunt Pru and Aunt Charity's. Damn.

Brandon slapped his cheeks once sharply to be certain that the phony smile he'd kept firmly in place while dealing with the wealthy-travelers-with-an-attitude was no longer in evidence.

Cripe, he thought, shaking his head, those people had been obnoxious to the maximum. They'd ended up canceling their reservation at Hamilton House in a huff and demanding the use of the telephone to call the other upscale hotels in town.

"Then the worm turned," Brandon said aloud as he continued his upward trek.

There had been no vacancies anywhere in Prescott. The couple had been forced to ask if they could re-instate their reservation at Hamilton House.

He'd softened their defeat by presenting them with a dozen cinnamon rolls from the hotel kitchen to take with them as they surprised their family with their early arrival.

"In their grungy clothes," he muttered. "Serves them right."

Enough of this, he ordered himself. It was time to refocus, direct his energies on Andrea, the aunts, breakfast, and the exchanging of Christmas presents.

Then the minute he could politely whisk Andrea away without hurting the aunts' feelings, he would get her alone and ask her to marry him.

Man, oh, man, this was going to be one fantastic

Christmas Day that he would most definitely never forget.

This was the epitome of that saying, "This is the first day of the rest of your life." A glorious life. A rich, warm, overflowing-with-love-and-happiness life. With Andrea.

Andrea Cunningham Hamilton. Mrs. Brandon Hamilton. Brandon and Andrea Hamilton. Yes!

Brandon quickened his step as he arrived on the fifth floor. The smile on his face was genuine as he greeted Aunt Pru when she answered his knock on the door.

"Merry Christmas, dear," Aunt Pru said. "Come in, come in. Andrea is already here, and breakfast is ready."

"Merry Christmas, Aunt Pru," he said, kissing her on the cheek.

He crossed the room to Aunt Charity and repeated the greeting and kiss.

"Merry, merry, big boy," Aunt Charity said.

Brandon turned and met Andrea's gaze.

"Good morning," he said, smiling. "And Merry Christmas."

"Yes, it is," she said, matching his smile. "A *very* Merry Christmas."

"You look festive," Brandon said.

Andrea glanced down at the bright green sweater she wore with winter-white slacks.

"String some lights on me," she said, laughing, "and I could pass for a Christmas tree."

Brandon had a sudden image in his mind of a holiday tree with its stiff, unyielding branches, followed immediately by the vision of a naked Andrea in his arms, soft and feminine, fitting perfectly against him.

"No," he said, then cleared his throat as heat shot through him. "You're definitely not a tree."

"Breakfast is served," Aunt Pru said.

The four were soon consuming scrambled eggs, bacon, toast and fresh fruit.

"We cooked this ourselves," Aunt Charity said. "Take a good look at it, because it isn't going to happen again. I'm thoroughly spoiled by eating in the hotel dining room, and this is the last of slaving in the kitchen."

"Hear, hear," Brandon said, raising his coffee cup in salute.

"We were having a delightful conversation with Andrea when you arrived, Brandon," Aunt Pru said. "About the possibility of adding specialty shops in the lobby. Tell him about it, Andrea."

"We were just chatting," Andrea said with a little shrug. "The lobby is enormous. There's room for three, maybe four, small shops."

"Go on," Brandon said, nodding. "You have my full attention."

"You don't want to distract from the decor in any way," she said. "The stores should have open fronts to give a visual flow from the lobby. You could have old-fashioned lampposts by each one, and maybe a cobblestone path in front, like a Victorian village, of sorts."

"I'm getting the picture," Brandon said. "What kind of stores are you thinking of?"

Andrea laughed. "I'll bill you for my advertising expertise, Mr. Hamilton." She paused. "You're targeting impulse buying. A flower shop for sending flowers to the wife in the room, or the one left at home by a traveling salesman. Flowers delivered to visiting guests.''

''Makes excellent sense,'' Brandon said, reaching for another slice of toast. ''What else?''

''Maybe candy,'' Andrea said, then took a sip of coffee. ''Marketing studies have shown that men will spend more impulsively than women while away from home. So, I'd also suggest some kind of exclusive women's wear. Sweaters, lingerie—whatever— for that away-from-home man to purchase for his sweetie pie.''

''Very interesting,'' Brandon said.

''The advertising would be very crucial,'' Andrea went on, leaning slightly toward him. ''These shops will be small, offshoots for owners who are well-established elsewhere. You pitch them as a service. You know…now you can have Bertha Burp Chocolates at your fingertips, right here in Hamilton House.''

'' 'Bertha Burp Chocolates'?'' Brandon said with a burst of laughter.

''I pulled that out of the air,'' Andrea said, smiling. ''But you get the idea.''

''I certainly do. I'm going to mull this over, then maybe have a powwow with my accountant, Clem Sinclair, about it.'' Brandon paused. ''Andrea, you're very good at what you do, aren't you?'' he said, his smile fading as he looked directly at her.

''Yes,'' she said, lifting her chin. ''I am. I wouldn't be the vice president of Challenge Advertising if I didn't excel in my profession.''

''But it exhausts you so, Andrea, dear,'' Aunt Pru said. ''It saddens me to think of the condition you were in when you arrived here.''

"Advertising is a very high-stress, demanding career," Andrea said.

"It wouldn't have to be if it was done on a smaller scale," Brandon said. Right here in smaller-scale Prescott, Arizona. "Pass the jelly, please."

"Challenge is growing all the time," Andrea said. "It's certainly not going to get any smaller if we maintain our level of excellence."

"Mmm." Brandon smiled at her pleasantly. "The jelly is by your right hand."

"There's more to life than just work," Aunt Charity said.

Bless you, Aunt Charity, Brandon thought.

"Yes, well…" Andrea said, picking up the dish of jelly.

But work was all she had in Phoenix, she mused. There was nothing else, no one else, to occupy her mind, her time. Her heart? Oh, for heaven's sake, where had that poor-little-me thought come from? Her life in Phoenix was busy and fulfilling, all that she wanted and needed.

Wasn't it?

Andrea, stop it right this minute, she ordered herself. Her brain was going off on a ridiculous tangent. Enough of this.

"Jelly," she said, offering the dish to Brandon.

The conversation shifted to the previous night's party. Andrea made comments in the appropriate places, smiled, and agreed that the event had been a huge success.

But a part of her was frantically pushing away the strange dark cloud that once again was hovering over her.

"Leave the mess on the table," Aunt Charity said

as the four got to their feet after the meal ended. "Pru and I will tend to it later. I want to open presents."

"She's like this every year, Andrea," Brandon said, chuckling. "She usually harps at me to chew faster so she can get to the gifts. She was on her best behavior during breakfast because you were here."

"Well, what are Christmas presents for, hotshot," Aunt Charity said, "if not to be opened? I'm ready to check out my loot."

They moved into the living room, Andrea and Brandon sitting on the sofa, Aunt Pru and Aunt Charity each settling in their favorite chair.

"Brandon, I put gifts under the tree for Ben, Jennifer, and Joey," Andrea said.

"They'll come by to say howdy at some point today," he said. "It was nice of you to remember them."

"Ben, Taylor, Jennifer, and Joey are part of our little family," Aunt Pru said, "which is getting delightfully bigger all the time."

Meaning what? Andrea wondered. That *she* was now being considered a member of the family? What a lovely and wonderful thought.

A family.

She hadn't had a real family since her parents were killed when she was four years old. She could no longer even remember what her mother and father looked like.

A family. For one more week. That was it, the length of time she could wrap the warm sentiment around herself like a comforting blanket.

Then...poof...it would be gone, when she left this special place, to return to where she belonged.

But she'd enjoy the idea of having a family while she was still here.

Andrea shot a quick glance at Brandon.

And, oh, yes, she thought, she would savor the lovemaking shared with Brandon Hamilton during the remainder of her stay in Prescott.

"I suppose you bought out the stores again for Joey," Brandon said, bringing Andrea from her thoughts.

"Of course," Aunt Charity said with a sniff. "Christmas is for children, isn't it?"

Brandon laughed. "And for aunties who like presents as much as kids do."

"Watch your mouth, big stuff," Aunt Charity said. "I'm old, and that gives me license to be as eccentric as I please." She rubbed her hands together. "Brandon, you're Santa Claus. Pass out the goodies."

The fun began.

A pile of brightly colored paper and bows started to grow on the floor as the presents were opened, accompanied by the appropriate exclamations of delight, along with heartfelt thank-yous.

Brandon gave the aunts cashmere shawls and lilac-scented dusting powder. The aunts had selected a gleaming, leather briefcase for Brandon, and a coffee table book about Prescott for Andrea.

"How lovely," Andrea said, running her hand gently over the dustcover of the book. "Look, Brandon, they put a picture of the town square in summer on the cover. There's the courthouse and that charming gazebo."

"Nice," he said, nodding. "I bet you don't see that many trees in bloom in one place in Phoenix."

"Not very often," she said, laughing.

"We wanted you to have pictures, memories, of our little town," Aunt Pru said. "It's also our way of saying how happy we are that you came here so we could get to know you."

"Thank you so much," Andrea said, smiling at them warmly. "I'll treasure this always."

"Well, let's see, here," Brandon said, reaching for two small gifts. "Here's one for Aunt Pru from Andrea and one for Aunt Charity."

The women accepted the presents from Brandon, opened them, then Aunt Pru beamed.

"Perfect," she said. "Absolutely perfect. This tells me that your heart is heading in exactly the direction I was positive it was going."

"Pardon me?" Andrea said, obviously confused by Aunt Pru's reaction to the gift.

"Enough said for now on that subject, Pru," Charity said. "Thank you, Andrea."

"Yes, thank you, dear," Aunt Pru said. "More than I can ever begin to say in words."

"Prudence, hush," Charity said.

"I've missed something, haven't I?" Andrea said, looking at Brandon. "This is all going right over the top of my head."

Brandon chuckled. "Well, you gave the aunts little crystal butterflies mounted on stands. It would appear that the butterflies just might be dancing."

"Dancing?" Andrea said. "I think they're supposed to look like they're flying."

"No," Brandon said. "They're definitely..."

"Dancing," Brandon, Aunt Pru and Aunt Charity said in unison.

"Whatever," Andrea said, her eyes widening at the

trio's outburst. "Okay, the butterflies are dancing. I'm glad you like them."

"More important," Aunt Pru said, "is the fact that *you* picked them out, dear. You chose the butterflies dancing over all the others."

"Hush, Prudence," Charity said again. "Just put a cork in it."

Still confused, Andrea shook her head slightly, then watched as the aunts opened the music boxes they'd purchased for each other and that she and Brandon had picked up at the store. She hadn't actually seen the boxes since they'd already been in shopping bags.

"Oh, they're exactly the same," she said, smiling. "What a coincidence."

"No, it isn't," Brandon said. "This happens continually. I've lost count of how many times they've bought the same thing for each other, without having been given one clue beforehand."

"Fascinating," Andrea said. "Do you think it happens because you're twins?"

"We believe it's because we love each other," Prudence said, smiling gently.

"Yes," Andrea said, nodding. "That's much nicer than some scientific explanation."

Brandon placed a box on Andrea's lap, then picked up another that he held at eye level.

"What's the scoop?" Aunt Charity said.

"These are the presents that Andrea and I bought for each other," Brandon said.

"Go for it," Aunt Charity said.

The Christmassy bows and paper were removed, the lids taken from the boxes, then tissue brushed aside. At precisely the same moment, both Andrea and Brandon lifted out their gifts.

Andrea gasped in surprise.

A wide smile broke across Brandon's face.

They had given each other the exact same thing.

A perky snowman was encased in a wafer-thin glass ball about the size of an orange. The base of the statue was shining teak wood.

When Andrea tipped the statue over, then back, snow fell in a silvery cascade, like a multitude of tiny, sparkling diamonds, just as it did in Brandon's.

A warm flush stained Andrea's cheeks and she kept her gaze riveted on the snowman, while striving to regain her composure.

The same gift, she thought. Just like the aunts had done. They were all looking at her, she just knew they were, because everyone, including herself, was remembering what Aunt Pru had said, that the purchase of matching presents wasn't a coincidence. It was because of love, deep abiding love.

"Thank you," Brandon said quietly, tracing one thumb gently across Andrea's cheek.

She shifted her gaze slowly to meet his, her heart seeming to skip a beat when she saw the warmth and the—what was that?—radiating from Brandon's dark eyes.

"And I thank..." Andrea started, then stopped speaking as unexpected and very unwelcome tears closed her throat.

"You're welcome," Brandon said.

The room, the aunts, the colorful debris on the floor, faded into oblivion as they continued to gaze into each other's eyes.

The telephone shrilled, breaking the sensuous spell weaving over, around and through Andrea and Brandon. She jerked at the insistent noise, then blinked as the room came back into focus.

Brandon sat the snow statue carefully on the sofa cushion and got to his feet.

"Now what?" he said, then cleared his throat as he heard the gritty quality of his voice. "I've already dealt with the travelers from hell this morning."

He crossed the room and snatched up the receiver in the middle of the fourth ring.

"Hello?" he said. "Yes, she is here with us... Who?... Hold on a second." He turned to look at Andrea. "There is a call for you from a Jack Jacobs, who says it's imperative that he speak with you."

Andrea nearly jumped to her feet, holding the snow statue in both hands.

"Jack is my boss, the owner and president of Challenge Advertising," she said, frowning.

"Perhaps he wishes to say Merry Christmas to you, dear," Aunt Pru said.

"No," Andrea said, shaking her head. "Jack wouldn't do that. He'd hardly even remember it was Christmas if it weren't for the fact that all the employees didn't show up today at the office. If he's calling, it definitely has something to do with work."

"Don't accept the call," Brandon said gruffly. "I'll have Ryan at the front desk tell him you couldn't be located."

"No, I have to speak with Jack," Andrea said.

"Andrea," Brandon said, "no."

"I have to, Brandon. It must be important for Jack to have tracked me down at Hamilton House. I didn't tell him where I was staying in Prescott, just that I was coming up here."

"Damn it, Andrea," Brandon said none too quietly. "It's Christmas Day."

"Damn it, Brandon," Andrea said, her eyes flashing as she matched his volume. "I realize that. But I'm going to take that telephone call. My career comes first!"

Ten

The silence that hung over the living room after Andrea's outburst was so heavy and chilling it was nearly palpable.

"I'm sorry," she said, pressing one hand to her forehead. "I didn't mean to shout at you, Brandon, but please understand that I have to take that call. I must speak with Jack."

She threw up her hands in a helpless gesture.

"Jack has been a widower for many years, you see, and has no children. Challenge Advertising is his baby, his life. It wouldn't occur to him that telephoning me on Christmas Day would be an imposition, but he'd consider my refusing the call as insubordination.

"I'm accustomed to his quirks. He often calls me in the middle of the night when he has a sudden idea he wants to share."

Andrea sighed.

"I'm babbling," she said. "I'm just trying to make you understand why I can't ignore that call."

"I understand perfectly," Brandon said, his voice low and flat. "Your career comes first. You can't make it any plainer than that, Andrea."

"But—"

"I'm sure my aunts won't mind if you go into one of their bedrooms," Brandon went on. "I'll have the call put through to here. There are phones by the beds in each of the rooms. Pick one."

"But... Yes, all right," Andrea said softly, then looked at the aunts. "I apologize for the intrusion on your Christmas."

"It is your Christmas, too, dear," Aunt Pru said gently.

"And I can't remember when I've had such a lovely one," Andrea said, producing a small smile. "If you'll excuse me, I'll just go into the other room and... Thank you."

Andrea nearly ran into the first bedroom she saw as she rushed from the living room, wanting to escape from the crackling tension.

She'd glanced quickly at Brandon as she passed him, and noticed the tight set to his jaw, the anger and some other undefinable emotion radiating from his dark eyes.

The telephone next to the bed rang and Andrea picked up the receiver.

"Hello, Jack," she said, forcing a light, cheery tone into her voice. "Merry Christmas. What is going on in that mighty mind of yours today?"

Brandon walked slowly over to the sofa, sank onto it, then sat back, staring at the ceiling.

"Hell," he said.

"You've got that straight, big boy," Aunt Charity said. "This situation with Andrea and her career is even worse than I thought."

She clicked her tongue in disgust.

"Imagine that odious man calling Andrea on Christmas," she continued. "Not only that, Andrea is supposed to be resting for two full weeks. That little tidbit obviously slipped Jack the Jerk's mind, too. What a dud." She paused. "You've definitely got your work cut out for you, hotshot, in spades."

"I love Andrea," Brandon said quietly, still staring at the ceiling. "I'm honest-to-goodness, forever and ever, in love for the first time in my life."

"We're very aware of that, dear," Aunt Pru said. "And we're so thrilled."

"Oh, yeah?" Brandon raised his head and looked at her. "I'm glad *you're* thrilled, because *I'm* beginning to think that I've made a tremendous mistake."

"Don't be silly," Aunt Pru said. "Andrea is in love with you, just as you are with her. I do believe, however, that she might not realize it yet."

"Or refuses to acknowledge it," Aunt Charity said.

"Bingo," Brandon said, lunging to his feet. He began to pace across the sections of the floor not covered with paper, bows and presents. "It must be nice to have a button to push to shut off emotions that are inconvenient."

He slouched back onto the sofa.

"You heard what she said. Her career comes first." Brandon narrowed his eyes. "Yep, that damnable career comes first. Always has, always will. Damn it, that woman stole my heart and I want it back!''

''Shame on you,'' Aunt Charity said. ''You're giving up without a fight? What kind of Hamilton are you? Snap out of it, or I'll smack your butt.''

''Brandon, dear,'' Aunt Pru said, ''have you actually told Andrea that you're in love with her? That you wish to marry her?''

''Don't assume too much, Pru,'' Aunt Charity said. ''Hot stuff here might have had plans to just shack up with Andrea.''

''Thanks a helluva lot, Aunt Charity,'' Brandon said. ''Of course, I want to marry Andrea. And, no, Aunt Pru, I haven't had a chance to sit her down to tell her how I feel and to ask her to become my wife.''

''Well,'' Aunt Pru said, folding her hands in her lap and smiling. ''That's the first order of business, isn't it?''

''What's the point?'' Brandon grumbled.

''Definitely going to smack his butt,'' Aunt Charity said, nodding.

''Brandon,'' Aunt Pru said. ''You *must* tell her how you feel.''

''Amen to that,'' Charity said.

Brandon dragged a hand through his hair. ''Maybe you're right.''

''We're always right,'' Aunt Charity said.

''And I have another full week to convince Andrea of how I feel,'' Brandon said.

''Yes, dear,'' Prudence said.

''Seven days,'' he said.

''And nights,'' Aunt Charity said, examining the fingernails of one hand. ''Just like last night.''

''What?'' Brandon said, his eyes widening.

"Give me a break, big boy," Aunt Charity said. "I wasn't born yesterday, you know."

"Charity, dear," Prudence said, "I do believe that perhaps you're overstepping just a teensy, tiny bit."

"More like a country mile," Brandon said, glaring at Charity. "Cripe."

"So sue me," Aunt Charity said, folding her arms over her breasts.

"Charity, dear, do be still for a moment, please," Prudence said. "Brandon, are we in agreement? You'll speak with Andrea as soon as possible?"

Brandon took a deep breath, let it out slowly, then nodded.

"Yes," he said.

"Splendid," Aunt Pru said, beaming.

Brandon closed his eyes, pressed his thumbs against them and tapped his fingertips against his forehead.

"I don't believe this," he said. "I'm thirty-five years old and I'm running to my aunts for advice like a fifteen-year-old adolescent with his first hormone-induced crush on a cheerleader. It doesn't do much for my macho ego."

"Don't be so hard on yourself, dear," Aunt Pru said. "This is the first time you've been in love. Age has nothing to do with knowing what is best. I respect you more for being willing to listen to advice."

"Just don't blow it," Aunt Charity said, then paused. "The way I did."

Brandon dropped his hands from his face and stared at Aunt Charity.

"What?" he said.

"There was a young man," Aunt Charity said quietly, "who I loved so very, very much. He came courting, but I was being coy, playing hard to get, because it tickled my fancy. I was having too much fun being the center of his attention to settle the matter by telling him how I felt about him.''

''What happened?'' Brandon said.

''I intended to accept his proposal of marriage the first time he came home on leave from the war,'' Aunt Charity said. ''But he didn't come home. He was killed in action. He never knew that I loved him with all my heart. He never knew.''

''Oh, Aunt Charity,'' Brandon said, shaking his head. ''I'm so sorry.''

''Don't make the mistake I did, sweetheart,'' Aunt Charity said. ''Tell Andrea that you're in love with her. Tell her, Brandon.''

Before Brandon could reply, Andrea came back into the living room. Brandon got to his feet and turned to look at her.

''Well, I…um…well,'' Andrea said, then wrapped her hands around her elbows.

''Yes?'' Brandon said.

''I guess you could say it's good news and bad news,'' she said, attempting to produce a smile that failed to materialize. ''The owner of a Chicago company we've been trying to get as a client came to Phoenix for Christmas and stayed at Jack's house. Jack managed to convince the man to let us put together an advertising package for him to review.''

''Go on,'' Brandon said, hardly breathing.

''The man agreed, with the stipulation that I head up the team, because he was aware of some of my other projects. It's a real feather in my cap.''

''Oh,'' Brandon said, then for the life of him

couldn't think of another thing to say as a knot twisted painfully in his gut.

"That's the good news," Andrea said. "The bad news is…" She took a wobbly breath. "I have to leave Prescott today to be able to meet with the man first thing tomorrow morning."

No! Brandon's mind thundered. Andrea was supposed to stay another week in Prescott. He was to have had seven more days—and nights—to convince her that he sincerely loved her, to show her how they could have it all, if she'd agree to be his wife.

Andrea loved him, damn it, he knew she did. Everyone who had seen the photograph in the newspaper knew that. How could she just stand there and calmly announce that she was leaving?

Because she doesn't know that *you* love *her,* idiot, a voice in his head hollered.

He had to calm down, regain control of his raging emotions, take this slow and easy.

"I see," he said. "Well, I guess congratulations are in order, Andrea. What kind of company does this big-shot guy own?"

"Cat food," she said, smiling weakly. "He wants a whole new image for his—" Andrea cleared her throat and lifted her chin "—cat food."

He was competing with cat food? Brandon thought incredulously, feeling his temper gaining force. Andrea was walking out of his life for cat food?

"Cat food is…is important," Aunt Charity said, narrowing her eyes and staring at Brandon. "To cats…and their owners. I'm sure it's a very competitive market, trying to please those cats. Right, Brandon?"

"Oh, yes, right," he said, nodding. "You bet. Cats

are finicky little buggers. It will take a dynamite advertising campaign to get those cats—the people who own them, that is—to try a different brand of... Hell,'' he said, shaking his head. "Cat food.''

"I apologize for cutting short our Christmas celebration,'' Andrea said to the aunts, "but I really must go pack. I can't begin to thank you for making me feel so special, so welcome, all week. And this truly was the nicest Christmas I've ever had.''

Andrea crossed the room to kiss Aunt Pru and Aunt Charity on their cheeks.

"Goodbye,'' Andrea said, struggling against her threatening tears. "Thank you.''

"It was wonderful having you with us, dear,'' Aunt Pru said.

"Yep, it was,'' Aunt Charity said. "Brandon, go help Andrea pack.''

"Oh, I don't...'' Andrea started.

"The quicker you pack, the sooner you can leave for Phoenix,'' Aunt Charity said. "You can start thinking about cat food during the drive down to the valley.''

Brandon placed Andrea's snow statue carefully in the box, picked it up, then scooped the large book into his other hand.

"Off we go,'' he said, forcing a lightness to his voice that definitely didn't reflect his mood. "You're going to have a heck of a time packing, Andrea. You're leaving with a lot more than you came with.''

Including an aching heart, Andrea thought, starting toward the door.

She didn't want to leave. Not yet.

She didn't want to say good-bye to Brandon. Not yet.

She didn't want to face the fact that she'd never see him again. Not yet.

But she had no choice, she told herself firmly. Duty called. She couldn't refuse to return to Phoenix earlier than she'd planned.

The possibility of winning over this potential client was a major step up in her career, especially since the client had personally requested that she put together his advertising package.

And her career came first.

Inside Andrea's room, Brandon set the Christmas gifts on the top of the dresser, while Andrea retrieved her suitcase from the closet. She flung it on the bed and opened it. She stared at it for a long moment, then turned to look at Brandon where he stood across the room.

"Brandon," she said softly, her voice trembling slightly. "I hope you realize that this isn't how I wanted things to be, my leaving Prescott earlier than I had planned."

"No?" he said, raising one eyebrow.

Andrea wrapped her hands around her elbows. "No. What we shared last night was…was beautiful, very special. I envisioned the week ahead…the days, the nights…as being so wonderful, as we created more memories to keep."

"But you're leaving," he said, nothing readable in the expression on his face.

"I have no choice but to go," she said, her voice rising slightly. "It's no different than your not being next to me when I woke up this morning because you had an emergency to tend to in the hotel."

"I went down to the lobby, Andrea. I didn't leave town."

"The principle is the same. Surely you can understand that."

"Up to a point," he said, nodding. "However, there is something that you don't understand."

Brandon closed the distance between them and gripped Andrea's shoulders. She dropped her arms to her sides.

"Andrea Cunningham," Brandon said, looking directly into her eyes. "I love you. I have fallen deeply and forever in love with you. I also believe that you're in love with me. I'm asking you to marry me, to be my wife, to stay with me here in Prescott."

Andrea couldn't breathe.

A strange buzzing noise echoed in her ears and funny little dots danced before her eyes. She took a sharp breath, shook her head and stared at Brandon.

"Pardon me?" she whispered.

"You heard me," he said, smiling at her warmly. "I love you. Ah, Andrea, don't you see? We can have it all. We can. A life together, children, a home. You can still have your career, too, only it will be on a smaller scale, that's all. Say yes. Agree to be my wife. Tell me you love me as much as I love you."

Voices began to hum in Andrea's mind, then gained volume, shouting at her in a jumble of words, messages, that tumbled one into the next, none of them discernible.

A chill coursed through her, followed by icy fear. Close behind came the dark sense of déjà vu that she'd registered before and didn't understand then, or now.

"No," she said, stepping back and forcing Brandon to release her. "No, don't say that. Don't say that you love me."

Brandon frowned. "Why not? It's true. It took me a while to figure it out, because I've never been in love before, but I am most definitely in love with you." He paused. "And you love me."

"No." Andrea shook her head as tears filled her eyes.

"Andrea, come on," Brandon said. "Everyone who saw the photograph in the newspaper knows that you love me. It was there, in your eyes, on your face, for all to see."

Andrea pressed trembling fingertips to her lips to stifle a sob.

"And there's also the matter of the butterflies," Brandon went on. "You chose butterflies dancing as gifts for the aunts. I thought at first that the butterfly business was just two dear old ladies' blathering nonsense. But now? I believe every word."

"I don't understand," Andrea said shifting her fingertips to her throbbing temples. "What about the butterflies?"

"When someone is in love, the butterflies dance," Brandon said, looking at her intently. "They truly do. You picked those crystal butterflies over all the other choices you had because they were calling to you. You're a woman in love. With me."

"No, I'm not," she said, a frantic edge to her voice as tears spilled onto her pale cheeks. "I can't be. I won't be. I'm not. You're reading far too much into a picture in the paper and Christmas presents I just happened to give to the aunts. I care for you very much, Brandon, *but I am not in love with you.*"

The sudden twisting pain in Brandon's gut traveled upward to encircle his heart. He wanted to rage in anger, demand that Andrea acknowledge her love for him. He wanted to beg, plead, with her to look deep within herself and embrace her true feelings for him.

Because, damn it, Andrea Cunningham *was* in love with him.

The evidence was all there, including their lovemaking that was beyond description in its beauty and intimacy.

"I'm sorry if I hurt you, Brandon," Andrea said, dashing the tears from her cheeks. "I thought we both realized we had a measured number of days to be together, then I would leave and it would all be over. Like…like Cinderella at the ball."

"You can't be serious," he said, his jaw tightening. "That's all this was to you? A fling? An affair? A hop in the hay?" Brandon dragged one hand through his hair. "No, I don't buy it. That's not how you truly feel."

"Damn it, Brandon," she said, fresh tears filling her eyes. "Quit telling me how I feel. I'm a woman, not a machine you can program to suit you. I'm being as honest with you as I can possibly be."

Brandon stared at her, trying to push past the excruciating pain of hearing Andrea declare so adamantly that she didn't love him. He struggled to clear his mind.

His future—their future—was at stake.

"What you should do, Andrea," he said, his voice not quite steady, "is ask if you're being honest with *yourself*." He narrowed his eyes. "What are you afraid of? Tell me. What is it?"

"Nothing," she said, nearly shrieking. "I'm not *afraid* of anything. Why can't you just accept the truth as it is? Brandon, please go. Leave me alone. I didn't want things to end this way, but you're not allowing me any other choice. Go. Just go.''

Brandon's hands curled into fists at his sides as he fought the urge to haul Andrea into his arms and kiss her to disprove the words she was speaking. Words he could not—would not—believe.

Don't do it, Hamilton, he ordered himself. He had to get a grip. He had to give Andrea some time to digest what he'd told her.

He had to turn around and walk out of that room.

Brandon took a deep, shuddering breath.

"All right," he said quietly. "I'll go. I'll leave you alone."

He strode to the door, then turned to look at Andrea.

"But, Andrea? Nothing can erase what I've said to you, how I feel about you. I love you with all my heart. Remember that. Think about it.

"Square off against your fears and find the truth within you. Please. Do that, Andrea, please, for us, for what we can have together for the rest of our lives. I love you, Andrea Cunningham, and I always will."

Brandon left the room, closing the door behind him with a quiet click.

Andrea stumbled to the bed, covered her face with her hands and wept.

Eleven

What are you afraid of?

I love you, Andrea Cunningham, and I always will... What are you afraid of? I'm asking you to marry me, to be my wife, to stay with me here in Prescott... What are you afraid of? We can have it all. A life together, children, a home. What are you afraid of?

What are you afraid of?

"Oh, stop," Andrea said aloud, pressing her fingertips to her aching forehead.

"Pardon me?" a young man said, looking over at where Andrea sat at the head of a long, gleaming table.

"What?" Andrea said. "Oh, I'm sorry, Richard. I didn't realize I'd spoken out loud. I was talking to...my headache. Yes, that's what I was doing. Silly, huh?"

"Tell me if it works," Richard said, smiling. "My head is killing me. Too much coffee and too little sleep, I guess."

"No joke," a pretty young woman said. "We've been going at this full steam since the day after Christmas."

"You're a great team," Andrea said, smiling at the group, comprised of two men and two women. "I picked you for this project because I know we'll come up with the perfect package for this prospective client. When we land this account, it will look very good in your personnel files."

"That's what I keep saying to myself," Richard said. "But, cripe, it's New Year's Eve. We're supposed to be out partying, lifting a glass of champagne to celebrate the arrival of a new year.

"But where are we? Sitting here at eight o'clock at night, trying to come up with idea number three for cat food. I hate cats. I really do."

"So do I," one of the women said. "At this point, I don't give a rip what the dumb things eat. The owner of that company rejected our first two proposals without even hearing them all the way through. This is hopeless."

"No, it's not," Andrea said, leaning forward. "We'll hit the mark, I know we will." She paused. "I intended to give you all tonight off, but Jack vetoed that. He's taking the prospective client out for a late dinner, then stopping by here afterward to see what we have."

"Oh, great, super," Richard said. "What we have is zip, zero, nada."

Andrea sank back in her chair and sighed.

What a hideous week this had been, she thought.

The hours at work had been long and grueling, the stress and pressure building with each passing day as she and her team attempted to please the cat food man.

And the nights? She'd spent those tossing and turning in her bed, reliving the final scene with Brandon over and over.

What are you afraid of?

And now, she thought dismally, the haunting echo of Brandon's words were following her to the office, creeping into her exhausted mind like insidious creatures determined to torment her.

I love you, Andrea Cunningham, and I always will.

Incredible. Brandon Hamilton was in love with her, had asked her to be his wife, to spend the remainder of her days by his side.

Yes, it was incredible. Incredibly wonderful and... Terrifying.

What are you afraid of?

Of all the things that were said on that final day in Prescott, why, why, why, did that question continue to beat unmercifully against her mind, her heart, her very soul?

Why, when she focused on it, even for a moment, did she register that chilling, dark sense of déjà vu? Dear heaven, what did that mean?

"Falling leaves," a woman said.

Andrea blinked, bringing herself back to the problem at hand.

"Falling leaves, Mary Ann?" she said. "What are you thinking regarding leaves?"

"Okay," Mary Ann said. "The cat man rejected our cats dressed up like people and going grocery shopping. He also did a thumbs-down on cartoon cats.''

"He did, indeed," Andrea said, frowning.

"So, try this," Mary Ann said. "We go for class, subtle and quiet. We have layered, misty clips of actual cats doing their thing. You know, running through a field of wildflowers, two of them tumbling around as they play, another standing on its hind legs batting at falling leaves that float just out of its reach.''

"Don't stop now," Andrea said. "This is marvelous. What else?''

"There's soft music playing," Mary Ann went on. "Maybe we even show all the clips in slow motion. And the end, we line up the cats in front of bowls and a voice-over says, 'At the end of a busy day, don't settle for less than excellence...Yucky Cat Food.'''

"Dynamite," Andrea said, getting to her feet.

Everyone started talking at once, their fatigue and discouragement forgotten.

"Let's sketch it out," Andrea said. "Mary Ann, you're a genius. Except...I think that instead of falling leaves, we should have butterflies. I would...really like...there to be butterflies.'' She shook her head sharply. "Yes. Well. This is the one, people, I just know it is. Don't consider that champagne toast at midnight out of the question, Richard. I think we're going to be celebrating, after all.''

Ben Rizzoli strolled up to the registration desk at Hamilton House, crossed his arms on the top of the counter and stared at Brandon.

"You look like hell," Ben said.

"Thanks, pal," Brandon said, glaring at him. "I'm so glad you stopped by to inform me of that fact. Yep, thanks a heap."

"You're very welcome," Ben said. "You're not sleeping well, are you? Aunt Pru told me that your appetite is shot, too."

Brandon shrugged.

"You haven't heard one word from Andrea since she left Prescott?" Ben asked.

Brandon sighed. "No. I'm trying to be patient, but…"

He shook his head.

"I think it's time for some action, Ben. I'm going crazy sitting around waiting for Andrea to figure out what she wants."

"Action it is, then," Ben said, smacking the counter with the palm of one hand. He paused. "What kind of action?"

"Damned if I know," Brandon said. "Flowers? A singing telegram? Candy?"

"Been there, done that," Ben said. "That's cliché, Brandon. You can do better than that."

"Oh, yeah? Like what?" Brandon dragged a hand through his hair. "My instincts, which probably aren't worth squat, tell me that I should be with Andrea, to make it impossible for her to ignore me and what we mean to each other."

"Do it." Ben glanced at his watch. "It's eight o'clock. You can be in Phoenix in less than two hours. Get Andrea's home address off her registration card and go for it. I'll cover the desk here."

"It's New Year's Eve, Ben. Andrea is probably at a party." Brandon frowned. "She sure as hell better not be at a party with some yo-yo. That woman is in love with *me*.''

''I know that. You know that. Everyone in Prescott who saw the photograph in the newspaper knows that. Andrea Cunningham just needs a little nudge to know that. Go nudge her. Oh, and take the address for that advertising firm she works for, too.''

''She wouldn't be there on New Year's Eve.''

''Don't be so certain of that, Brandon. She left here on Christmas Day because the head honcho of that outfit told her to.''

''Yes, you're right.'' Brandon frowned. ''I don't know, Ben. I don't want to blow this.''

''Go, Hamilton.''

''You're right, Rizzoli. I'm outta here.'' Brandon punched Ben on the arm. ''Thanks, buddy.''

''You bet.''

Ben watched as Brandon strode toward the elevator.

''Good luck, my friend,'' Ben said quietly.

Andrea and her team worked feverishly to create a presentation of Mary Ann's new idea. Cats at play were sketched out roughly on large sheets of transparent paper so an overlay effect could be achieved.

Richard and Susie went down the hall to another room to hopefully find the perfect music from the available inventory.

Andrea's head was buzzing from fatigue, and she ached from head to toe as she pushed on.

She was in the process, she thought dismally, of totally erasing all the renewed vim, vigor and energy she'd replenished while in Prescott.

She was drained, both mentally and physically.

This week of never-ending work hours, combined with the emotional upheaval regarding Brandon, had cost her dearly. She was so tired she could weep. She just wanted to put her head down on the table and wail.

Just before eleven o'clock, the presentation had been mounted on fiberboard backing and placed on a wooden easel. The tape of the chosen music was in a player, waiting for the proper button to be pushed.

They were ready.

The entire team appeared pale with dark smudges of fatigue beneath their eyes. Even Susie's ever-present smile was nowhere in evidence.

"We did it," Andrea said. "You're wonderful, absolutely terrific, all of you."

"We're wiped out is what we are," Richard said, rotating his neck back and forth.

"When Jack said he was taking that guy for a late dinner," Mary Ann said, "he wasn't kidding. Look at the time."

"The cat food man is being royally wined and dined," Andrea said. "He's a bachelor and obviously likes the party life. Jack has been taking him to fancy restaurants and nightclubs all week."

"Must be nice," Richard said. "But I'd settle for one New Year's Eve party."

"Well…" Andrea said, massaging her aching temples. "It's up to you. You certainly deserve to be here to help present this package, but if you'd prefer to go, it's absolutely fine with me. There's no reason for all of us to be bringing in the new year pitching an ad campaign for cat food."

"I'm gone," Richard said. "Good luck, Andrea."

"Forget partying," Susie said. "All I want to see is my comfy bed."

The others agreed that enough was enough. With wishes for success with the presentation and for having a happy New Year, the four made a hasty exit.

Andrea stood in the empty, quiet room, weaving slightly on her feet as a wave of dizziness and nausea assaulted her. She glanced longingly at her chair at the head of the table, then dismissed the thought of sitting down in fear that she'd be unable to rise to her feet again.

"Hurry up, Jack," she muttered. "How much wining and dining can two men do in one evening?"

Andrea began to roam around the large room, mentally rehearsing the presentation she would give.

Somehow, she thought, she had to come across with bubbling enthusiasm, sound as though she was so excited about the crummy cat food that she could hardly contain herself. Her team deserved her very best performance.

What did *she* deserve? she thought. Even more, what did she really want in her life, her future? She missed Brandon with an intensity that was staggering, overwhelming. She yearned to see his smile, hear his laughter, be the recipient of his magnificent kisses, engage in exquisite lovemaking with him.

"Andrea, don't. Not now," she said aloud, still trekking around the room.

It was foolish to dwell on Brandon when she needed every ounce of energy she could muster to concentrate on the presentation for the cat food.

Cat food, she thought. How ridiculous. She was a physical and mental wreck. She was alone an hour before the beginning of a new year, all because of cat food? Did that make sense?

Yes, yes, of course, it did. This was her chosen profession, the career she was dedicated to. It brought her monetary rewards. It gave her fulfillment.

Didn't it?

"I'm very fulfilled," she said, then frowned. "Aren't I?"

Oh, forget it, she thought in the next instant. She was too exhausted to think about fulfillment, or lack of same.

Cat food. All she could handle dealing with at the moment was that damnable cat food.

The sound of men's voices reached her and she hurried to stand next to the easel.

Smile, Andrea, she told herself. Look peppy and proud, excited and enthused to the max. Smile.

Jack and a portly man in his late fifties entered the room.

"There she is," Jack said, beaming. "The best advertising executive in the west, second only to me. Where's your team, Andrea?"

"They did such a marvelous job," she said, "that I sent them on their way. This is their work as much as mine, though. In fact, this fantastic presentation was Mary Ann's idea."

"Yes, well, whatever," Jack said, flipping one hand in the air. "Are you ready to present it to Bert, here?"

"Yes, I am," she said.

"All right, little girl," Bert said, sinking heavily onto a chair. "Show me what you have. I hope it's better than the others. They were a great disappointment to me, you know. So?"

So, eat a worm, little boy, Andrea thought, narrowing her eyes as she stared at Bert.

"Andrea?" Jack said.

"What? Oh. Yes. I'm very excited about this package," she said. "It's some of the finest work ever produced by my team."

"Get on with it," Bert said, then yawned.

Don't murder him, Andrea told herself. The man isn't worth going to jail for.

"Fine," she said. "Now, then…"

Andrea gave a brief overview of the philosophy of the ad campaign, then turned and pressed the button on the tape player, producing music that was a lovely combination of quiet and upbeat.

"The cats would be shown," she went on, hearing the thread of exhaustion in her voice, "in subdued shades of color, surrounded by a soft golden, or perhaps pink, glow. The images would merge, blend, one into the next as the kittens play, romp, even snooze and—"

"That's it in a nutshell," Bert said, throwing up his hands. "Snooze. You're putting me to sleep, little girl. I can't sell cat food to people who are no longer awake."

He got to his feet.

"I've seen enough," he said. "This is junk. Hellfire, shut off that damn funeral music."

Andrea pushed the stop button on the player with a shaking finger. A red haze of fury flashed before her mental vision, taking the place of the sudden tears that had filled her eyes.

"I've been with the same advertising agency for thirty years," Bert said, hiking up his pants over his bulging belly. "And I'm going to stay put. You people have offered me nothing remotely close to fresh and inspired ideas.''

He shook his head.

''I'm flying back to Chicago tomorrow and renew my contract with the outfit I know I can trust to produce something I can use. Lord, a slow-motion cat trying to smack a butterfly? Hell.''

It was too much, it really was.

Andrea was trembling with fury and fatigue. Everything seemed to come crashing down on her at once, nearly crushing her with the intensity of emotions tumbling one into the next.

Along with the anger at Bert and her physical weariness was the heartache and confusion about Brandon, the chilling loneliness the image of him in her mind caused to course throughout her.

And there, too, was the strange, menacing dark cloud of déjà vu, the sense of having somehow lived this scenario before.

Andrea blinked, shook her head slightly, then a gasp escaped from her lips.

The darkness in her mind's eyes was suddenly lifted, revealing vivid scenes from her childhood in the foster homes. Painful memories slammed against her like punishing blows.

She heard the voices of people fawning over her, saying how pretty and well-mannered she was.

She heard them promise, *promise,* to start proceedings to adopt her, so they could take her home to be their cherished daughter.

She heard the foster mother of the moment telling her that the people had changed their minds, were not going to adopt her after all.

Over and over it happened. Promises made. Promises broken. Hopes and dreams shattered time and again. Trust and belief in the future destroyed.

So she'd learned—oh, yes, she'd learned—to bury her emotions deep within her, to leave them untouched, beyond her reach. She protected her heart, mind, her very soul, against the heartache of love.

Promises made. Promises broken.

Dear God, what had they done to her? What had she become?

She became aware of Jack attempting to placate Bert, telling him that Andrea and her team would start over in the morning on a brand new advertising package to present to him.

"No," Andrea said. "No, we won't."

"Yes, you will," Jack said, looking at her intently.

Andrea stumbled forward to grip the back of a chair to keep her legs from crumbling beneath her.

"You never even considered switching ad agencies, did you, Bert?" she said, her voice quivering. "This has all been a sham, a way for you to escape the Chicago winter for a while and be wined and dined in warm, sunny Phoenix. Your coming here represented a promise to view our presentations with an open mind. That was a promise you never intended to keep. Isn't that right, Bert? Isn't it?"

"Andrea, that will do," Jack said sternly.

"Let me tell you something, Mr. Cat Food Man," Andrea went on, as though her boss hadn't spoken. "You did me a tremendous favor. Your actions enabled me to discover something about myself that I didn't even know."

Tears spilled onto Andrea's pale cheeks.

"And guess what, Bert?" she said, a sob catching in her throat. "The butterflies in that scene with the cat weren't flying—*they were dancing*. How do I know that? Because I'm a woman who is in love with the most magnificent man in the world. In love. Only people in love can make the butterflies dance.''

"Andrea," Jack said, "you're out of control."

"Oh, no," she said, shaking her head. "I'm in control for the first time since I was a child. I'm in love, and I pray to the heavens that I'm not too late, that I haven't lost the man who loves me in return."

"You haven't lost him," a deep voice said. "He's right here."

Brandon strode into the room and Andrea stared at him with wide eyes, wondering frantically if she was imagining that he was actually there.

"Who in the hell are you?" Jack said.

Brandon went to Andrea, gripped her shoulders and looked directly into her eyes.

"Me?" Brandon said, his gaze riveted on Andrea. "I'm the man who loves this woman with every breath in my body. I'm the man, who along with Andrea, can see the butterflies dancing."

"Enough of this nonsense," Bert said. "I'm leaving. Thanks for the freebies, Jack, you dumb patsy."

"What?" Jack said. "Is what Andrea said true? You never intended to consider changing agencies?"

"Hell, no," Bert said. "My outfit suits me just fine. I flew out here to party in the sunshine and let you pick up the tab. See ya." Bert sketched a salute and left the room.

"That lousy…" Jack started, then looked at Andrea. "Andrea, sweetheart, go home, get some rest, take tomorrow off. You can get cracking on a different account the next day."

"No, Jack," she said, "because I quit. If you want to sue me for breaking my contract, then go for it."

"But… Ah, hell, forget it," Jack said. "Butterflies dancing? They deserve each other. They're both crazy." He stomped from the room.

Brandon watched Jack leave, took a shuddering breath, then looked directly into Andrea's eyes.

"Andrea Cunningham," he said, his voice not quite steady, "will you marry me? Be my wife? The mother of my children? Live with me in Prescott?"

"Yes, oh, yes," she said, tears streaming down her face.

She threw her arms around Brandon's neck and he encircled her slender body with his arms, pulling her close to him.

"I'm so sorry, Brandon," she said, sobbing. "I was terrified to love you, to trust in you and your love, in your promises. Forgive me, please, for hurting you. I'll explain it all to you later, but please believe me when I say that I've laid my ghosts to rest at long last. The future is ours. Forever."

"Ah, Andrea," Brandon said.

She smiled at him through her tears. "I love you so much, Brandon Hamilton."

"And I love you, Andrea Cunningham," he said, his voice choked with emotion.

The sound of car horns honking and bells ringing reached them.

"It's midnight," Andrea said.

Brandon cradled her face in his hands. "Happy New Year, my love."

"Happy forever years," she whispered.

Then Brandon lowered his head and captured Andrea's mouth with a kiss that sealed that commitment as it chased the shadow of hurt and loneliness into oblivion.

Brandon broke the kiss. "Let's get out of here."

"Yes," Andrea said. "I'll come back tomorrow and collect my personal belongings from my office. We can spend the night at my apartment." She paused, a thoughtful expression on her face. "That's all it is, just an apartment. What you and I will have together will be a home, a real home, overflowing with love."

Brandon slid one arm across Andrea's shoulders and tucked her close to his side.

"Wait," she said.

She went to the easel and removed the drawing of the cat and the butterflies. She rolled it into a tube and nodded.

"I want to keep this," she said, smiling.

"We'll frame it," Brandon said, matching her smile. "Come on. We should be outside greeting the new year, saying hello to the first day of the rest of our lives together."

Several hours later, Andrea woke with a start, then gasped in dismay when she looked at the clock.

Three-sixteen in the morning, she thought. She'd fallen asleep while Brandon had taken a shower. She'd intended to wait for him, eagerly anticipating the exquisite lovemaking they would share. But her exhaustion had won out and she'd fallen asleep!

She turned her head, a soft smile forming on her lips as she saw Brandon sleeping peacefully next to her, visible in the glow from the night-light she kept in the bathroom.

Oh, how she loved him, she thought. Their future

together was spread out before them like a lush array of yet unopened Christmas presents. Did Brandon know, really know, how much she loved him?

"Maybe I'd better show him," she said aloud.

Andrea eased onto her stomach and began to wiggle her way closer to Brandon, inch by inch. As she moved, she could feel the heat of desire begin to thrum low within her naked body.

Brandon's arm shot out and snagged Andrea around the waist, causing her to gasp in surprise. He scooped her up as though she weighed no more than a feather and settled her on top of him.

"And just where do you think you're going?" he said, smiling at her.

"You scared the bejeebers out of me," she said, matching his smile. "I was traveling over here to seduce you."

"Can't be done."

"Is that a fact?"

"Yep," he said, chuckling. "For you to seduce me would mean that I was resisting your womanly charms until you convinced me otherwise. I haven't got a resisting bone in my body."

"How nice."

Andrea lowered her head and claimed Brandon's mouth in a searing kiss, her tongue delving between his lips to seek and find his tongue.

A groan rumbled in Brandon's chest as he rolled over, catching his weight on his forearms. He deepened the kiss and Andrea's lashes drifted down. She savored the feel of him, the taste, the heat of passion licking throughout her like burning flames.

She felt so vibrantly alive, she thought dreamily.

So young, carefree and happy. She was in love. And, oh, it was glorious.

Brandon broke the kiss and shifted to one of Andrea's breasts, laving it with his tongue, then paying homage to the other.

As Andrea's hands roamed over Brandon's broad back, she rejoiced in the strength of this man, the power, tempered with gentleness.

They kissed and caressed, remembering, anticipating, as their desires soared. Brandon trailed nibbling little kisses across Andrea's stomach, then down... down. She tossed her head restlessly on the pillow, whispering Brandon's name, until she could bear no more.

"Brandon, please," she said, her voice a near sob.

He moved up, then into her, meshing their bodies into one miraculous entity.

"Oh, yes," she murmured, lifting her hips to meet him.

The rocking rhythm began, gaining force, thundering into a tempo that was wild and earthy, evidence of their want and need. Upward they flew, reaching for the exquisite release, together.

"Brandon!"

They were there, bursting into their private place in shattering ecstasy, hurled seconds apart into the kaleidoscope of brilliant colors.

And...

Butterflies.

There was a multitude of beautiful butterflies and all of them, every single one, were dancing.

They drifted back, sated, spent. Brandon sank heavily next to Andrea on the bed and wrapped one arm around her waist, his lips resting lightly on her temple. Their breathing quieted and heartbeats slowed.

"Did you see them, Brandon?" Andrea said, awe and wonder ringing in her voice. "Did you see the butterflies dancing?"

"Oh, yes, I saw them," he said. "They were incredible."

"And ours."

Brandon sighed in contentment. "Forever."

Epilogue

They were married in the church where Brandon's parents had exchanged wedding vows decades before.

An announcement was placed in the Prescott newspaper, stating that Mr. and Mrs. Brandon Hamilton were now husband and wife and were living in Hamilton House until they found the perfect home to purchase. A reception would be held in the spring, on the town square, so that everyone who wished to, could attend the celebration.

Andrea walked behind the reservation counter and poked Brandon in the ribs.

"Hello," he said, dropping a quick kiss on her lips. "How did it go?"

"I now have my fourth client," she said, smiling. "I'm going to put together an advertising package for your friend who owns the store where I bought my spiffy red coat."

"Which matches your spiffy red car," Brandon said. "Mickey is out there washing your mean machine. I think he's working up to asking you if he can drive it again." He paused. "Congratulations on signing client four to a contract."

"Thank you," Andrea said, dipping her head. "I'm very pleased. Four is today's lucky number. This is our four month anniversary."

"So it is," Brandon said, pulling her into his arms. "Happy anniversary, Mrs. Hamilton."

"Same to you, Mr. Hamilton."

"Hey," a deep voice said. "No hanky-panky on the job, you two. Knock it off."

Andrea and Brandon nearly jumped apart, then Brandon smiled.

"Taylor! My, gosh, man, how long has it been? Andrea, this is the Taylor Sinclair you've been hearing rotten things about. Taylor's father, Clem, is my accountant, remember? Taylor, this is Andrea, my wife of four months."

"My sympathies, Andrea," Taylor said.

Andrea laughed as she registered the fact that here was yet another extremely handsome man who had grown up in Prescott.

Taylor Sinclair was tall and well-built. But while Brandon and Ben had dark hair, Taylor's was varying shades of brown and sun-streaked blond. He had rugged features and expressive brown eyes.

The dynamic duo of Brandon and Ben, Andrea mused, was now the terrific trio with the addition of Taylor.

"I'm here on official business," Taylor said, bringing Andrea back to attention.

"Oh?" Brandon said.

Taylor frowned. "My father isn't well, Brandon.

You know he had to move down to Phoenix because the doctors said the altitude up here in Prescott wasn't good for his heart condition.''

Brandon nodded.

"Well," Taylor went on, "he made it through the grueling income tax season, but he has finally admitted that he's ready to hang it up. I moved to Phoenix from San Francisco to be near my dad and to take over his accounting business. I'm calling on all of his clients to determine if my stepping in is acceptable."

"Well, sure, that's fine," Brandon said. "But I'm sorry that Clem isn't up to par."

"He should live a long time if he takes it easy," Taylor said. "He claims he's ready for the retirement scene, but we'll see how he adjusts to idle hours."

"Give him my best," Brandon said.

"You bet," Taylor said.

"Listen, Taylor, I'm glad you came up from the valley," Brandon said. "Andrea and I would like to sit down with you and discuss the possibility of adding some specialty shops in the lobby of Hamilton House. We want to have a financial view of the idea."

"Sounds interesting," Taylor said, nodding. "Let's look at some numbers."

"Well, hotshot," a familiar voice said. "It's about time you surfaced like the bad penny you are."

Taylor turned and a wide smile broke across his face.

"Aunt Charity," he said, holding out his arms. "And Aunt Pru. Come give me a hug."

The sisters moved into Taylor's embrace, then stepped back again.

"You're looking good, big boy," Aunt Charity said, scrutinizing Taylor from head to toe. "Are you married?"

Taylor laughed. "No. I'm footloose and fancy-free, Aunt Charity, which is exactly the way I like it."

"For now, dear," Aunt Pru said sweetly. "But perhaps you'll change your mind on the subject in the future, just as Brandon did."

"Nope," Taylor said, shaking his head. "Not me."

"Prudence," Charity said, "we've got our work cut out for us. Ben, Jennifer, and now hunk-of-stuff Taylor, here have no business going through life alone."

"Uh-oh," Brandon said.

"I thoroughly agree with you, Aunt Pru, Aunt Charity," Andrea said decisively.

"All in good time," Aunt Pru said. "All in good time. And there's one thing we don't have to be concerned about."

The group looked at her questioningly.

"The butterflies," Aunt Pru said serenely. "For those in love, there is a magical and endless parade of butterflies dancing."

*   *   *   *   *

Taylor Sinclair believed marriage was for fools, but he reconsiders when he falls for Janice Jennings—a secretly stunning woman who hides behind a frumpy disguise. A barrier Taylor vows to breach....

In July 1999, discover why appearances are deceiving when bestselling author Joan Elliott Pickart's miniseries,

THE BACHELOR BET, *continues with*

THE IRRESISTIBLE MR. SINCLAIR, Special Edition #1256.